Stowaway to Eden

Mardy Burke

Second Edition

Printed in the United States of America via Lulu
Press (www.lulu.com)

ISBN: 978-0-615-20991-3

I would like to thank you, Amanda, for all your help. Your encouragement and positive comments kept me going. I love you!

Stowaway to Eden

At Home in Eden

Return to Eden

United in Eden

Chapter One

Lauren pressed her ear against the door that joined her hotel room to her uncle's. She listened for any sign of movement before she cautiously opened it a crack to see if he was there. With him nowhere in sight, she held her breath and opened the door wider to look around the entire room. It was empty. She had no doubt he was downstairs in the smoke filled saloon trying his luck at cards.

His opened window allowed off-key piano music and a woman's high pitched giggle to fill the room. Her uncle had left one lantern burning low giving the room some light but not much. She needed to maneuver to the window without knocking into anything. She didn't want to alert Prather who was posted in the hall. He was hired to keep an eye on her and to make sure she didn't leave. He was like an ever present shadow, lurking nearby wherever she went. Lauren wasn't going to let him or anyone else stop her from carrying out her carefully thought out plan. All she wanted was to leave the wretched town and her greedy uncle.

Her uncle's window was on the alley side which made it perfect for escape. The alley was dark enough to conceal her in the shadows. How to reach the ground without breaking her leg or neck posed a slight problem. Making her way to the window, she measured the distance to the ground.

"Not too far..."

Their rooms were on the second floor. Though it wasn't too high, it was still too dangerous to jump. Lauren noticed a down spout within reach. She pushed against it to make sure it was secured tightly to the building. She tossed her small bundle to the ground below to free both hands before hoisting herself upon the window sill. Trying to keep her balance on the tiny ledge, she reached for the spout. The braces holding it against the building were barely big enough to secure her foot. She was determined to make it work.

"Lord, send your angels to keep me safe," she whispered. Drawing a deep breath, she let go of the window and grabbed the spout with both hands. Her foot slipped off of the brace leaving her hanging on for dear life. With both legs dangling, she searched blindly for the brace with her toes but couldn't find it. She squeezed the spout as tight as she could with her knees. She looked over her shoulder to size up the distance between her and the ground. The only thing she could do now was drop. If she rolled when she hit the ground it would lessen the chance of broken bones.

"Here goes nothing." She closed her eyes before she let go. It felt like an eternity before her feet hit the ground. She fell flat on her back knocking the wind out of her. She gasped for air as she lay looking up at the starry sky.

"Easy, relax...short breaths..."

A dog bark, alarmed by the noise from her fall. Lauren slowly sat up when she was able to catch her breath and moved her legs to make sure she wasn't hurt. Her back side felt bruised but she was thankful she landed on it and not her head! The noise in the saloon was so loud she was sure no one had heard the ruckus she made.

Lauren pressed as close to the building as she could to hide in the dark shadow it offered. Her heart was pounding so hard she could hear it roaring in her ears.

"Please Lord; please don't let them find me." Leaning her head back she tried to control her labored breathing. Her legs were shaking so badly she was afraid her knees would buckle. The moon's rays were hidden behind the clouds. She slowly made her way toward the back of the building and poked her head around the corner. No one was on the street. Staying close to the buildings she made her way to the livery at the end of town.

Lauren opened a small door in the rear of the building. In the darkness the smell of horses and hay filled her senses as she slipped through the door. She stood in silence while her eyes adjusted to the low light. With the darkness surrounding her she felt invisible and a little more at ease. She sat on a bale of hay to get some control over her nerves. A nudge to her shoulder caused her to jump to her feet. She turned quickly to see big brown eyes staring back at her. With a friendly whinny the horse nodded his head up and down. With a sigh of relief she stroked the horse's soft nose. Realizing it was one of the matched bays she saw earlier. She moved to the next stall and found the other horse.

"The wagon should be in here!" She remembered a man at the mercantile said he was going to store it in here tonight. The moon's light filtered between boards revealing a heavily loaded wagon. Lauren smiled. Where it was headed she didn't care. All she knew was she had to get out of this town without being detected.

The cargo was covered with a heavy tarp. It was tied down so tight, she wasn't sure she'd be able to slip under it without leaving evidence of tampering. She walked around and tugged on it until she found a loose corner. She slid her small frame under the tarp and carefully shifted the cargo so she could lie down. Lauren tried to get as comfortable as possible with the crates and only God knew what else was jabbing and poking her. It was going to be a long night. She tucked the small bundle she brought under her head for a pillow. As she started to relax she thought of her parents and how she missed them since their death. How could God take them away from her? How could He allow her to end up running for her life? She started to cry. She was alone and scared; never before in her twenty years had she felt so abandoned. What was she going to do?

"Lord, I don't know where this will lead me. I thank you for helping me get this far. I ask that you continue to lead me and protect me. Watch over me tonight my Jesus."

After praying she felt a sense of peace flow through her. She closed her eyes and gave into a restless sleep.

Chapter Two

"Good morning Kyle! It's a beaut out there today. It'll make my trip a little nicer." Caleb whistled as he slapped the livery owner on the back.

"Morn'n Caleb. You're all hitched and ready to go. I hope the weather stays good for ya. This time of year you never know what it'll do. I remember one year....." Kyle started with one of his stories.

"I'd love to hear the story friend but I better get on. Pa's expecting me at the end of the week. He knows we can take care of ourselves but he still tends to get concerned when we run behind. You can tell me your tale the next time I'm around."

"Guess your right. You tell your Pa I send my *hellos* and he need not make a stranger of himself. You boys are old enough to take care of things and let him have a break now and then."

"I'll do that, take care of yourself!" With a smile Caleb jumped in the driver's seat.

Kyle opened the doors wide so Caleb could get on his way.

"Hi ya! Come on boys!"

With a slap of the reins the team jolted forward. They were ready to stretch their legs and head home. Caleb was ready for home too. He didn't mind the trip but he hated being away from his family. He was the oldest of four boys. It was his job to ride to Hadley twice a year to take care of ranch business.

William Whitworth, Caleb's pa, believed his boys needed to know how to run the ranch so there would always be someone there to take it over if anything should happen to him. Once he felt comfortable with their knowledge of the ranch the business aspects would fall in place.

Jake, William's second born, would go to Hadley if needed but he'd rather stay home and work the range.

Evan, the oldest twin, was content with whatever was put before him and welcomed a challenge which usually got him into trouble.

Ethan, the youngest of the boys loved the ranch but had different plans for his future. But, at seventeen, his pa didn't think he was old enough to know what he wanted.

Caleb's thoughts were turned away from his family when he saw the sheriff and a man he didn't recognize signaling for him stop.

"Whoa boys, ho now." The bays were not happy at having to stop so soon. They knew the direction they were headed was toward home and they wanted to get there as anxiously as their driver.

"Ho Buck!" Caleb commanded again.

Buck pawed impatiently at the ground showing he was not happy with the delay.

"Morning Robert, is there a problem?" Caleb asked while eyeing the stranger.

"This here is Henry Bailey. He's looking for his niece. Seems she slipped out last night and he can't find her."

"Why are you stopping me?" Caleb pushed his hat back on his head while he took a closer look at the aggravated man. The stranger had a dark scowl on his face.

"Maybe she had reasons to run away," Caleb said without averting his eyes from Bailey.

"And what are you implying, sir?" Bailey's face turned red with anger. "Take the tarp off your wagon. She's a sly one and I'll not have you towing her away." Bailey went to the back of the wagon and started pulling on the tarp.

"Hey! Get away from there!" Caleb jumped down from his seat and ran to Bailey's side. "Back off! There's no one hiding under there. I have this packed so full nothing or no one could fit back there."

"Take it easy Caleb, just move on back." Robert quickly stepped between Bailey and the wagon.

"Mr. Bailey, are you sure she didn't go to the diner to get something to eat? She could be at the mercantile shopping. You know how girls are, they…"

"She's not at the diner or mercantile!" Bailey hissed between clenched teeth. "She wouldn't take extra clothes with her to shop. She's run away I tell you!" He grew more excited as he continued angrily. "Ever since the death of her parents, I've had nothing but trouble with her. She's been left to me to care for and this is the thanks I get! I tell you one thing; as soon as I get my hands on her I'll show her a thing or two. Now get that tarp off and let me have a look!"

Lauren woke to the sound of arguing. When she felt the tugging on the tarp she froze with fright. Was that her uncle's voice? Was she so scared she imagined it? She tried not to breathe as she listened to the heated conversation.

"I can assure you, Mr. Bailey that she is not in my wagon. Maybe if you were more understanding to her situation she wouldn't have run," Caleb said while heading back to the front of the wagon.

"Why you..." Bailey started toward Caleb in a fury but Robert intercepted him before he could lash out at him.

"That's enough Bailey! Caleb said he didn't have her and I believe him now back off!" Robert yelled as he held Bailey at bay; his hand resting on the butt of his pistol.

"I can't imagine why she wanted to run. I feel for the girl if you're all she has left." With that said, Caleb jumped back in the wagon leaving Robert to handle the very irate Henry Bailey.

Lauren lay close to tears as fear ripped through her. She felt sick to her stomach and fought to keep her emotions under control. The angry voices of her uncle and the sheriff faded as the wagon made its way down the street and out of town. When she felt safe from harm she allowed the tears to flow trying her best to keep her sobs from being heard by the driver. She wasn't sure how long she cried but eventually the rocking of the wagon and the consistent clopping of the horses' hooves rocked her into a deep sleep.

She was jolted awake when the wagon wheel hit a hole. She was so sore and stiff from lying in the same position that every muscle and bone screamed for her to stretch. She heard the driver whistling and hoped he was deep in thought and wouldn't notice her as she slowly stretched one arm at a time then her legs. The cargo didn't allow much room to move let alone stretch. It helped ease the stiffness but now the sun was beating down on the tarp making it extremely hot. Lauren felt that if she didn't get some fresh air she'd die of suffocation. She reached for the tarp where she slipped under the night before and carefully lifted it just enough to let some air pass through. The opening was tiny but a small breeze managed to find its way in once in awhile to send a little comfort. She started to relax until she felt the driver turn the wagon off the road. Her mind started racing wondering if he was going to stop.

Caleb looked at the sun and determined by its position it had to be past noon. His stomach was agreeing. There was a creek not far ahead and he decided not to stop until they reached its banks. The team picked up speed as the scent of water hit their nostrils. They were at the creek within minutes.

"Whoa boys, ease up now," He pulled back on the reins until the bays stopped under the shade of a large tree. "That's it, how about a break? Don't know about you but I'm about starved to death."

He jumped down from the bench, unhitched the team and led them to the water. He let them take their fill and while they did he splashed the cool water over his cark, curly hair. He wet his handkerchief and tied the cool cloth around his neck. He tethered the horses so they could eat the dark green grass and rest. Caleb stretched his long arms and legs before inspecting the wagon. He tossed his hat to the side and was checking the ropes holding down the tarp when he noticed a small section in the back flapping in the breeze.

"Blast you, Bailey!" He spat. He had to undo all of the rope so he could tuck the loosened section under it in case it rained. He made his way around the wagon untying the rope until it dropped to the ground. He growled under his breath at the wasted time spent on the chore. A swift breeze caught the tarp and blew it off the wagon uncovering its contents. Caleb's usual easy - going temperament was quickly turning to impatience. He was tired, hot, and hungry and this was delaying his break. He tugged and pulled on the tarp to get it back in place but came to an abrupt stop when he saw something move in the back of the wagon. He quietly moved to the rear of the wagon and pulled the tarp back. He couldn't believe his eyes. Lying curled up against the side of the wagon was a girl.

Caleb was dumb founded and didn't know what to do. Suddenly, he realized she must be the girl Bailey was looking for and she was in fact in his wagon! His anger rose as the situation hit him full blast. Before he knew what he was doing he grabbed Lauren and yanked her out of the wagon. She let out a cry when her feet hit the ground. Her legs were so stiff they buckled under her and she fell to her knees. Caleb had a hold of her wrist as she went down.

"Noooo! Let go of me!" she screamed. "You're hurting me!" She pulled as hard as she could to free her arm but his grip was solid. "Let go of me!"

"Do you realize what you've done?" Caleb asked in a fury. He pulled her to her feet and grabbed her by the upper arms and made her look him directly in the face. Looking up at him was no girl but the most beautiful woman he'd ever seen. She had a tiny oval face framed in black curls. A long braid hung over her shoulder. Her eyes were wide with fright; their color caught his attention. He'd never seen bluer eyes in his life. He couldn't take his eyes off her and didn't realize that his grip loosened enough for her to almost jerk herself free. He came to his senses and tightened his hold on her. She was determined to get away and with every ounce of strength she could gather she kicked him in the shin.

"Ouch!" Caleb let go of her and grabbed his leg where the heel of her boot hit.

Lauren seized her chance and ran as fast as her sore legs allowed but it wasn't fast enough. Caleb was behind her in no time. He grabbed her braid pulling her against his chest.

She turned on him once again and started to kick like a wild cat. Afraid his legs would encounter another assault he turned her around and forced her to her knees. He had his arms around her pinning hers so she could no longer lash out and hit him.

"Let... go... of me!"

He held her so tight she could barely speak. "Not on your life! Not till I get to the bottom of this! Stop fighting me!" Caleb tried to calm his voice remembering the terrified look in her eyes. "I'm not going to hurt you."

She was completely exhausted and felt like she was going to pass out from lack of air. Lauren gave in to the tears and let them fall.

Caleb couldn't stand to hear her choked sobs. He felt her small frame shake causing him to feel guilty for treating her so rough. "I'm going to let go, please, don't run," he said. "I promise I won't hurt you. I just want to talk to you."

When he felt her relax, he slowly let her go and turned her to face him. She leaned forward to support her exhausted shaking frame. She had her arms wrapped around her mid section as she tried to control her sobs. She took deep breaths. She knew she was defeated and there was no way she could out run this man. She was at his mercy.

"Please, don't take me back," she whispered. "If you do; he'll kill me."

Caleb pulled his handkerchief from around his neck and handed it to Lauren. She slowly reached for it with a trembling hand. The cool cloth was refreshing against her hot, tear streaked face. "That's a pretty serious accusation," Caleb said while examining the long lashes that framed her pretty eyes. "Why don't we start from the beginning? Why would he want to kill you?"

"It all started when he showed up and asked my father for a job. He's an evil man and will do anything to get what he wants – even murder."

"What started when he arrived?" Caleb became intrigued with her and wanted to know more about this beautiful stowaway.

"When he first showed up he was actually very nice and I liked being around him. He begged my father for a job and because Henry used to work for a bank my father thought his experience would help with the books." She took a deep breath and pushed the damp hair from her face. "It went well for awhile until cargo started to disappear which he quickly blamed on a new deck hand. Then one day, my father and I were in his office and a deposit receipt was on the desk from the previous day. It had been altered. That's when the arguing began."

"You know that for a fact?" Caleb asked.

"Yes, you see, I also worked for my father when my mother would allow. I worked the previous day because Henry didn't show. I made out the deposit for that day and when I was about to take the money to the bank Henry arrived. Being the *gallant* uncle he pretended to be, he said it was not safe for me to carry the money so he took it." Lauren let out a heavy sigh. "He returned hours later drunk; carelessly leaving the altered deposit receipt on the desk. I found it the next day and showed it to my father."

"What did your pa do?" Caleb asked.

"He went to the bank with the receipt book but never made it there. He was found dead in an alley. The constable said it was robbery but I know it was Uncle Henry."

They sat in silence for a few minutes before Caleb continued with his questions.

"What about the receipt book? Was it with your pa when they found him?"

"No, it was never recovered."

"You still have no proof. What about your ma? Where was she when all this was taking place?"

"My mother was so heart broken after my father's death she became very withdrawn. There were decisions to be made and the business needed attention. She didn't know how to deal with it since my father saw to all our needs." Lauren lowered her eyes and continued in a soft voice. "My parents were so much in love...they were like one person. I think when father died she did too. She just stopped caring about everything." She was looking at Caleb now with questioning eyes. "Does that make sense?"

His stopped breathing when she looked at him so innocently.

"What am I going to do with her? How do I know this is all true?"

He didn't know what to think until he remembered when his own mother died. Yes, he knew exactly what she was talking about. He never forgot the far away look in his father's eyes when William thought he was alone. Even though Caleb was only eleven at the time he saw and felt his pa's pain. His pa was lost without his beloved Elizabeth. Eventually as time went by, William realized he had four boys that needed him and they were hurting too. He knew his wife wouldn't want him to neglect them and out of his love for her he buried his sorrow.

"Henry took advantage of mother's state of mind and used it to slither his way into her life." Lauren's voice brought Caleb back to the current conversation. "A few weeks after the funeral he started to call on her and then he'd bring her flowers and little things he knew she liked. Little by little he won her trust and within a year of my father's death he convinced her that she needed him to care for her. So she married him."

Lauren shivered in spite of the heat. She closed her eyes and wrapped her arms around herself. "I couldn't get her to listen to me or see him for the snake he really was. I think she was trying to recreate the love she had for my father through Henry. She missed him so much." Lauren sat in silence. A lone tear slid from beneath her closed eyes.

"I heard Henry say both your parents were dead. Tell me how she died – if it's not too painful to talk about," Caleb requested, hoping to shed some light on what he should do with her.

"Henry started bringing warm milk to her when she retired for the night. He told her it would help her relax and she would have sweet dreams. Every night it was the same thing and it wasn't long after his *loving* attentions that I noticed she'd have trouble rising in the morning." Her voice dripped with sarcasm. "I knew he was putting something in her milk so I asked her to stop drinking it. She did and she started to feel better."

"Surely she realized then what he was doing. What happened after she got better?" Caleb asked.

"It wasn't long before Henry noticed the change in her too and found out she wasn't drinking the milk. He was furious with her and with me when he found out I was the one who convinced her not to drink it. He told me if I ever meddled with his affairs again I'd be sorry." Lauren's shaky voice revealed fear.

"Did you report any of this to the authorities or try to get help?" Caleb asked confused.

"I tried but I was not allowed to leave the house alone or speak to anyone. He let our servants go and told mother that it was ridiculous to spend good money on work we could do ourselves. So, I didn't have anyone left at home to go to." Lauren looked at Caleb and saw doubt. "You don't believe me do you?" She started to get up but he pulled her back to the ground where she was sitting.

"How did your ma die?" he asked.

"One morning she just didn't wake up. She supposedly passed away in her sleep. I think Henry killed her but no one questioned it because she had been so sick."

Caleb didn't know what to say. He stood up and paced back and forth a few times before he stood in front of her. He pushed his hat back on his head and with a deep sigh he extended his hand to help her up.

"I'm not going back. You can leave me here if you want and go on your way but I am not going back!" The determined look on her face convinced him that she meant what she said.

"I won't take you back," he reassured her. "I don't know what I'm going to do with you right now but I promise, I won't be going back to Hadley." His stomach reminded him that he hadn't eaten since breakfast and imagined she was hungry too.

He finished fixing the tarp then put together a quick lunch while she freshened up by the creek. If she wanted to slip away while he was busy he'd let her – or would he?

That night Caleb lay on his back looking up at the twinkling stars. His hands were clasped behind his head adding little comfort from the hard ground beneath him. He'd been sleeping under the stars on cattle drives for the past twenty years. The outdoors was his second home. He decided not to continue on his journey after their conversation.

There had been little conversation earlier while they ate their meal. He was careful not to ask anymore questions about her past. He thought about the events that unfolded previously in the day and wasn't sure what to make of the woman that was sleeping on the other side of the fire. It took her some time before she finally relaxed and tended to her personal needs. He made camp and secured the wagon and horses for the night allowing her some privacy. He still had so many unanswered questions - including her name. He sat up annoyed with himself for being so foolish. He couldn't believe he didn't know it after spending the entire day with her!

He looked across the fire at the small woman sleeping soundly. She was lying on one end of a blanket while the other end was wrapped snuggly around her tiny form. Her head was resting on the small bundle she had brought with her. The flickering light from the fire cast a warm glow over her delicate facial features. Remembering the kick she gave him earlier, he decided never again to let a woman's size fool him. She was tiny but not frail by any means; the bruise on his shin was proof. If she stood on her toes he was sure her head wouldn't reach his shoulders. His pa always told him dynamite came in small packages. He wasn't joking.

He remembered her eyes, sky blue rimmed with long, dark lashes.

"The eyes are the windows to a person's soul," his ma would say with a twinkle in her own eyes. "If you look deep enough you'll see their brain!" she'd tease her boys.

This brought a smile to his face. He missed her, more now than ever. She'd know what to do about his unexpected package. He'd bring this stowaway home to her and pa and let them take care of the situation. He could then get on with his life.

Caleb settled back to try and get some rest. He had a long hard ride ahead of him. He wasn't sure what he was going to do with … with who?

"Caleb, you idiot!" he scolded himself once again. He let out a heavy sigh. *"I should have hog tied the girl and brought her back! What difference would it have made? Today's fiasco already delayed my arrival home. I should've sent her packing!"* Caleb was the problem solver of the family but this time he bit off more than he could chew. *"I'll leave her in the next town. It's not as big as Hadley but I'm sure she'll blend in and find work. From what she's mentioned, she's worked before so she must*

have some education. But what if everything she told me was true and Bailey is looking for her? Who'll be there for her? Stop! She's not your problem! Get a hold of yourself!" He rolled on his side and drew a blanket over his head. He tried to quiet his thoughts. *"I'll just sleep on it; tomorrow's another day for answers."*

With that decision he felt more at ease. He closed his eyes and tried to imagine the looks on his brothers' faces when he told his tale. They're the ones who usually brought chaos and mishaps home, especially the twins who were always trying to outdo each other. It seems big brother has the tale this time and they're not going to believe it!

****

Bailey sat at a table in the saloon with a glass of whisky in one hand and a map in the other.

"I've asked everyone in this town if they've seen her but, she's gone, sir."

Bailey's head shot up when Prather informed him of Lauren's disappearance. His steel eyes penetrated those of the tall, slender man.

Alex Prather was very crafty. Bailey liked his ways and decided he'd be a valuable asset for his plans. Prather had spent most of the day asking the residents and business owners of Hadley if they'd seen Lauren. To their disappointment, no one could recall seeing her, including the stage office clerk.

"There is no possible way she could just disappear!" Bailey barked.

He kept thinking about the wagon he had approached when he first discovered her missing. He cursed himself for not insisting on a search of its contents. The driver headed east when he left town. Without knowing where he was headed, Bailey had to second guess the destination. The next town on the map was a place called Jenkins.

"I've been looking at this map. I believe we should head to this town here." He pointed at it with a pudgy finger. "That's the direction that wagon headed. I believe our *future* was in there. We're not getting anywhere sitting around this place."

He folded the map and stuck it in his jacket pocket. The stage wasn't going to Jenkins for a week so he needed to purchase a couple of horses. The thought of having to spend what little money he had angered him further. He emptied his glass and slammed it on the table.

"*You spoiled wench! Just wait till I get my hands on you. I will find you if it's the last thing I do!*"

Chapter Three

"Hurry pa! She's getting pretty restless!" Ethan yelled. One of their mares was due to give birth at any moment. It wasn't an unusual event on the ranch; but always exciting. "Easy girl, you're doing fine, that's it, easy girl," Ethan spoke softly to the mare. He knew he couldn't show the excitement he felt or she'd sense it and become nervous. "Hold her head Ev. That's it, keep her still," he instructed his twin brother, Evan.

"Wish pa'd hurry, she's gonna have this little one before long," Evan remarked.

Will entered the barn with a bucket of warm water. He knelt down next to Ethan to inspect the mare's progress. "Yeah, she's good'n ready, keep her still Ev. Keep talking to her. Easy girl, easy now…" William spoke to her as he rolled up his sleeves. "Looks like I'm gonna have to help this little one along. Ethan, hold her tail back out of the way."

Will washed his arms up to the elbows and knelt down behind the mare. He had to move slowly so she wouldn't become excited. They couldn't take a chance of her hurting herself or one of them. He proceeded to search for the stubborn new born in the mare's birth canal.

"I think I found the problem. Feels like it's not… turned all the way. Let's see if we can help ya' little one," Will spoke aloud as if the foal could hear him.

Ethan was amazed at the patience his pa had with animals. Every move he made was slow but steady. He spoke to the mare consistently in a low soft voice. Suddenly, she let out a loud snort and jumped as Will helped pull the colt out by the front legs. Finally the head and body followed.

"He's not move'n pa, is he dead?" Ethan asked.

"Pa? Can I let her go?" Evan asked. His arms were getting tired.

"Let her go boys and stand back," Will instructed.

They jumped back as the mare rose. She turned to inspect the wet, bloody colt that lay motionless in the hay.

"Pa, what's wrong with him?" Ethan asked.

"Just hold on, give him a chance to come to his senses," Will answered.

The mare nudged the little brown colt with her nose. They all laughed when it let out a tiny whinny. The mare proceeded to clean him. Within minutes, he was standing on wobbly legs that didn't look strong enough to hold him.

"Ah, he's a fine one. Good job boys! Let's celebrate!" Will laughed heartily.

The three of them were headed to the house talking excitedly about the colt when they heard riders approaching. It was Jake and a couple of ranch hands.

"What's all the excitement?" Jake asked.

"Misty gave birth to a colt, a nice one too!" Evan answered.

"Great! I'll have to check in on them but right

now I'm starved. Trail food is about to do me in. Don't let Cook know I said that or he'll do me in!" he said as he dismounted.

"I got him Jake," Kent, the ranch foreman said as he took Jake's horse.

"Thanks, Kent. Hey, you all worked hard this past week. Enjoy your time off in town and stay out of trouble!" he warned them.

"We won't do anything you wouldn't!" Kent tossed over his shoulder.

"I know! That's what scares me!" Jake teased.

"Let's get cleaned up. We can catch up on everything while we eat," Will suggested.

"Sounds good to me?" How are things with you two?" Jake asked the twins.

"We've been busy around the house. Hey Pa, when will we get to go on the trail with Caleb and Jake? They were a lot younger when they went out the first time," Evan asked.

"We'll see, maybe the next time." Will answered.

"I'm in no hurry; I like the work around here just fine," Ethan said.

"You mean… you have more time to stick your nose in a book around here," Evan teased as he gave his younger brother a little push.

"At least I know how to read!" Ethan pushed back.

"You keep acting like that, you'll never go out," Will laughed.

"Aw, pa. We're just having fun," Evan told him.

"Come on, Annie's holding supper for us. She'll want to hear about our new addition." Will was hungry. He knew his boys were too. He had no doubt that their housekeeper,

Annie, would have a fine spread waiting for them.

Later that evening, after their stomachs were satisfied, they relaxed near a warm fire.

"A toast! To the safe return of my second oldest and the birth of a fine new colt!" Will held his glass up as he spoke. His boys followed suit.

"Here, here!" Jake added.

Soft tinkering filled the room as they tapped each others glasses. Will and Jake tossed their whisky down without a flinch. Evan and Ethan tried to keep up with the older two. They swallowed the liquor in one gulp and tried to stifle their coughs as it burned their throats.

"Another... toast!" Evan said in a raspy voice. He held out his glass for a refill.

"I don't think so, young man. One's enough for you," Will laughed.

"Aw Pa, I'm seventeen and ya still treat me like a baby," Evan said with his head hanging.

"Then stop pouting like one," Ethan scolded. That's all Evan needed as an excuse to jump his brother. Before Ethan knew what hit him they were both flying over the sofa and rolling on the floor.

"Alright! Break it up you two!" Will yelled.

He grabbed one boy and Jake grabbed the other. Arms and legs were still flying when they were pried apart.

"What's all this, now?" Annie flew out of the kitchen when she heard the commotion. "I declare! You lads 'bout gave me a heart attack!"

Will hired Annie after Elizabeth had passed

away. He needed help with the twins and she had been recently widowed.

She came to Eden two days after the twin's birth. She quickly became part of the family. They couldn't imagine life without Annie. She was large and jolly with thick Irish blood in her veins. It wasn't uncommon to see her after one of *"her boys"* with either a rolling pin or wooden spoon in hand.

The twin's temper died as they straightened their clothes. They hung their heads, looking at their shoes when Ethan started to laugh. Not able to hold back Evan soon joined him, then Will and Jake.

"For the life of me I'll nev'r figure you two out," Annie said shaking her head. "Fight'n one minute, laugh'n the next. Now don't you go leave'n this room a mess. I've been clean'n all day and I won't be hav'n you come in here like the cattle you own..." Annie continued her scolding as she returned to the kitchen. What else she said wasn't heard over the laughter.

"It's time for you two to turn in for the night. Fix the furniture before Annie tans your hides then get to bed," Will instructed.

"Yes sir," the twins answered in unison.

Will and Jake settled down with a cigar and coffee to wind down from the day's activities. The nights were getting cooler. The warmth from the fire was welcomed.

"What news did you hear from Caleb?" Jake asked.

"He sent a wire the other day and said business went well. All the supplies we needed were in. He should be home at the end of the

week if the weather permits."
Jake stretched his legs out in front of the fire and puffed on his cigar. "That's good. Good business, all the supplies were there… he had it made. Maybe I should have gone this time," Jake said.

If he knew what Caleb was dealing with at the moment he'd be very content where he was; in front of the fire sipping his coffee without a care in the world.

Chapter Four

Caleb stoked the camp fire after he woke. The night was cold and he wondered how his "guest" managed. He looked where he last saw her sleeping and found that she was no longer there. A big knot formed in his stomach. Not only was she gone but so was the bed roll and bundle she carried.

He jumped to his feet but couldn't move. He didn't know what to think. Horses – did she take one of the horses? He ran to the wagon and let out a sigh of relief when he saw both his bays where he left them the night before. He checked the wagon for tampering when he spotted a small mound under it near the back wheel. He hunkered down and found Lauren curled up in a tiny ball fast asleep. He let out a sigh of relief then gently shook her leg to wake her. Startled, Lauren quickly sat up, hitting her head on a steel bar.

"Aaaaa!" She grabbed her head with both hands and lay down. Lights flashed behind her closed eyes as pain shot through her temples.

"I'm sorry! I didn't mean to scare you!" Caleb didn't know what to do. He gently touched her shoulder. "Are you okay? Come here, let me take a look."

Lauren sat up holding the side of her head. She opened her eyes and saw concern on his face.

"I'll be fine, it's just a bump. I've had them before." She lightly rubbed the throbbing knot. "I'll feel better if you let me take a look, now move your hand out of the way," Caleb insisted.

Lauren let him part her hair and look at the swollen, red bump. He wet his handkerchief with water from his canteen and applied the cold compress to her head.

"Hold that there for awhile; it should help with the pain. I'll get some coffee started." He started to walk away but his curiosity got the best of him. "What are you doing under here?"

"I was afraid you'd leave without me so I thought if I slept here I'd hear you." She couldn't look at him she was so embarrassed.

"Or get yourself killed!" he exclaimed. *"So, she's not so tough after all."* He thought to himself. He tried to hide his smile as he extended his hand to her. "I'm Caleb Whitworth."

"Lauren, Lauren Bailey." She shook his hand.

"Well Lauren Bailey, I'd like to say it's been a pleasure but I think a more appropriate statement would be; it's been an adventure. I'm not going to leave you; so relax." He smiled and winked at her. He returned to the fire trying not to laugh.

They had their coffee, bacon and dry biscuits before Lauren excused herself. Caleb had the wagon hitched and was ready to get on the road but Lauren was still no where in sight. He didn't want to scare her again or interrupt her privacy so he quietly walked in the same direction he saw her leave. At first he thought he was imagining it but after a few more steps he realized he heard her talking. "Who could she be talking to?" he whispered. He silently moved a little closer.

"...I still don't know what you have planned for me but I will follow. I will lean on you during this time of need; you will be my mighty fortress. Forgive me, Lord when I fail you or don't trust you. Please, bless Mr. Whitworth for watching over me and oh yes, for not running over me. That was very stupid. Watch over us today as we travel. Amen."

She was praying! He hadn't heard anyone pray since his ma died. He felt as if he were intruding so he silently moved back to the wagon.

His ma used to read to them from her bible and take them to church. They didn't go back after she died. The adventures she read to them about David and Goliath and the battle of Jericho were the only things he remembered. It was just a book of stories, right? So then who was she talking to? God? He was taught God was good. If He was, why did he take his ma when he was so young? How could she pray to someone who allowed someone to kill her parents - *if* that was all true? With every hour he spent with this woman he became more confused.

Caleb's thoughts were interrupted when she emerged from the path.

"I'm sorry; did I keep you waiting long?" she asked. Her questioning blue eyes sent his heart racing.

"Actually I was just getting ready to call for you. Are you ready then?" He grabbed her hand and helped her to her seat.

She noticed the distracted look on his face. *"I've delayed him much too long again,"* she silently scolded herself for being so inconsiderate.

"Well, then, shall we see what's in store for us today? Get up boys!" He slapped the reins and the bays lunged forward.

The rising sun shot brilliant rays of light over the tree tops toward heaven. The horizon was a deep shade of red resembling flames behind the tree's dark silhouettes.

Lauren loved the sunrises. She viewed them as God's paintings. This particular morning brought scripture to mind.

"When it is evening, ye say, It will be fair weather: for the sky is red.
And in the morning, It will be foul weather to day: for the sky is red and lowring."

The couple traveled in silence for some time before Caleb noticed Lauren had closed her eyes. She was rubbing her head where she had bumped it.

"I'm so sorry about scaring you this morning. How bad is it hurting?" he asked.

"It's just throbbing a bit, it will be fine. It's not your fault, I should have - trusted you." Her cheeks turned a light pink.

Caleb didn't want to make her feel uncomfortable but he also needed to learn more about her and her situation. He was hoping to get to the next town early in the day. The businesses would still be open for job inquiries. He didn't want to just leave her stranded. It was a fair size town and he hoped he could help her find employment.

"What kind of education do you have?" he asked.

Lauren's temper sparked. Did he think she was an uneducated street urchin?

"I was tutored by the finest and then went to finishing school. I have a well rounded education, Mr. Whitworth."

The anger in her voice caught Caleb off guard. He shifted nervously in his seat.

Lauren realized how harsh her words were and felt horrible. She thought about her appearance. Her dress was torn and dirty and her hair probably looked like a rat's nest. What did this man really think? She let out a sigh. "I'm sorry; I didn't mean to bite your head off. Especially after the kindness you've shown me."

"No need to apologize." He thought about her schooling for a minute before continue. "I didn't know there was a finishing school in Hadley? I've been there quite often. I didn't realize it had so much to offer."

"Hadley? I'm not from Hadley. I'm from Cape Jennings, north of Hadley. My parents sent me away to finishing school. Cape Jennings is a very prosperous city but is *lacking in the area of finer schools* as my mother used to say. So, I was sent away to further my education."

"Cape Jennings is on the coast isn't it? I've heard of it but I've never been there." Caleb leaned back in his seat and propped one of his long legs on the wagon front. "What were you doing in Hadley?"

"I honestly don't know. My uncle informed me

he was going for business and I was to go with him. He was planning something but I don't think it had to do with the business. I know he was up to no good after I heard him speaking to a man outside of my hotel room one night. He thought I had retired for the evening but I couldn't sleep and I heard them talking. I tried to hear the conversation but they were whispering. I did manage to hear him say something about getting the money when the job was done. I panicked thinking that I was the job and he was planning to kill me. That's when I climbed out the window and hid in your wagon."

"You climbed out the window?" He was amazed at the lengths she went to get away. "You're lucky you didn't break your neck!"

"I just wanted to get out of there. I would have jumped from six stories if I had to." She let out a little laugh at the thought.

Caleb felt she was feeling a little more at ease with him so he continued with more questions.

"Was your father's business very prosperous?"

"I suppose it was. We didn't lack for anything and lived very comfortably. It's the only life I knew so I assume he was doing well. Why?" she asked.

"I was just asking." Caleb wondered what Lauren's father left behind financially and if that had anything to do with her uncle's plans. His thoughts were interrupted when he noticed the wind blowing harder. He turned to find a darkening sky behind them. "We need to make a shelter before the storm reaches us," he warned her.

They were traveling on open prairie with no protection against the quickly approaching storm. The deep rumble of thunder filled the air. Caleb stopped the team and jumped from the wagon.

"What are you doing? There's no shelter here." Lauren grew nervous as the dark clouds quickly approached.

"We'll have to make due with what we have, come on, get down." He offered his hand for assistance. Caleb pulled their blankets from their seats and tossed them under the wagon.

"What can I do to help?" Lauren asked.

"Get the water and something to eat and put it under the wagon then help me tie the horses to the side of the wagon. I don't want them bolting if they get scared, that would not be fun," he teased.

The wind started to blow in strong gusts. The thunder and lightning sounded like it was directly overhead. The rain started to fall in big drops and quickly turned to a downpour.

"Get under the wagon!" Caleb had to shout in order for Lauren to hear him above the wind and rain.

She quickly did as she was told and crawled under the wagon, Caleb was right behind her.

"Here, these will protect us a little." He handed her a blanket.

She wrapped it around her shoulders and leaned against the front axle. The wind was blowing so hard that the wagon and blankets did little to keep her dry.

"Sit over here next to me; I'll block some of the rain from hitting you." Caleb was leaning against one of the wheels. He put a dry corner of his blanket on the ground for her.

The time passed without any relief from the storm.
"We're going to have to stay here for the night." Caleb was discouraged; he wanted to get to the next town. "It's going to be cold and we obviously can't have a fire under here. I want you to stay close, it's the only heat we'll have through the night."
"Oh no!" Lauren yelled.
"I promise, I have no other intentions but to stay warm! That's all I meant," he clarified.
"No, I left my stuff on the bench! It's going to be ruined!" She started to crawl out from the safety wagon but Caleb grabbed her by the arm and pulled her back.
"Hold on! It's already too late; your clothes are already soaked. We'll lay them on the tarp when it stops raining and they'll dry. You don't need to get out there and get sick. That's all I need."
"I don't care about my clothes, it's my bible!" Lauren was near tears.
She was heart broken; it was a gift from her parents. They gave it to her the day she was baptized. It had once belonged to her grandmother.
Caleb couldn't understand why she was so upset over a book. He saw a single tear run down her cheek.
"You can get another one when we get to town," he said trying to comfort her.
She wrapped the blanket around her tighter and turned her back to him.

Caleb didn't know what he had said wrong. He was at a loss for words. It was just a book for goodness sake. He knew the mercantile sold them. Shoot! He'd buy it for her. That is of course, if they ever got there!

Rain or shine he needed to get to Jenkins to at least get a wire to his pa. He needed to let him know he was alright.

Chapter Five

Branding time on the Eden Ranch was a dreaded time but very crucial. There was no rest until every last calve bore the Eden brand. Will lifted the branding iron from a bellowing calf. The smoke and stench of the burning hair and hide assaulted his nose. He stood and stretched his aching back.

"Ooooee! I'm getting too old for this." He placed the iron in the coals to reheat for the next calf.

"You picked a perfect time to send Caleb out pa, you owe us big," Jake said. "I think a lynching is in order."

"You're right but I don't recall you reminding me we were so close to branding; so you're as much to blame." He was hot, sweaty and dirty and not in the mood for criticism.
Jake smiled at his irritated pa and got down from his horse. "Here, I'll take the iron for awhile old man."

"If I didn't need you so badly today I'd shoot you for calling me old," Will growled. "Ethan! Ev! Ride on in!" he shouted.

The boys recognized the edge in Will's voice and didn't waste time obeying.

"Ya pa?"

"I'm leaving for awhile and your brother's in charge. I don't want to hear that he had any trouble from the two of you. Do you understand me?"

"Yes sir," they answered in unison.

The boys exchanged looks and knew better then to argue when their pa was in one of his moods.

Will was normally an easy going, fun loving person but Jake's comment about Caleb's absence got him worrying about his oldest son. Will should have heard from him by now. He motioned for Jake to come to him.

"I'm going to town to see if there's a wire from Caleb. If you need me send one of the men."

"Will do, we'll be fine. We should have them branded by evening." Jake tried to relieve his pa's worries. "Caleb's fine pa, he'll be home soon."

"You're probably right but I'll feel better if I check." Will mounted his horse and gave a few more instructions before heading to town.

The ride to town was peaceful. He reflected on the many times he and his Elizabeth rode together to town. After the boys arrived, she didn't go as often. The two kept her busy always underfoot. The memories were good, he missed her so much. He was so deep in thought, he arrived in town before he knew it.

"Afternoon Will. What brings you to town? Thought it was branding time out your way?" Tim Poynter, the town sheriff, asked as Will stopped in front of telegraph office.

"I came to see if Caleb sent a wire, he usually sends one from the towns he stays in to keep me posted," Will explained. "I should have heard from him from Jenkins by now."

"The western stage arrived late today due to

weather. Said it was a bad one. I'm sure Caleb ran into the same problem. Check for a wire and come back to my office for some coffee. You look like you could use some," Tim offered.

"I'll do one better, meet me at Sally Ann's and I'll buy you lunch. I need real food," Will laughed heartily.

"Now how can I pass that up? I'll head over and get a table. You know how busy she gets this time of day." Tim headed to the café whistling.

Clayton's Creek hired Tim ten years ago as sheriff. He and his wife, Ruth, were from a big city and the town had concerns at first that hiring him would be a mistake. But, in the end, he proved to be a good man and a good sheriff. He and Ruth attended church every Sunday and helped everyone they could. They were admired by most. Will had a lot of pull when it came to keeping him. Tim never forgot how Will fought for him to stay in Clayton's Creek.

"Hello Nate, I was checking to see if you got a wire from Caleb. He's running late from his trip," Will said.

"No sir, the wires are down from a storm. I'm taking some men out tomorrow to find the disconnection. I heard it was a bad one, a tornado took out a farm not far from Jenkins."

Will's heart sank. He knew Caleb always stayed in Jenkins to help break up the trip.

"Okay, but if you do hear anything will you let me know as soon as possible?" he asked.

"Sure will and my wife and I'll be praying for your boy." Nate smiled as he went on with his work.

"Thanks." Will nodded his head in appreciation.

Will headed to the café with a heavy heart. All he could do was hope that Caleb was safe and he'd be home soon.

Chapter Six

The storm raged for most of the night making it difficult to sleep. By early morning they managed a couple hours of slumber as the raging winds and rains ceased.

Lauren, not realizing it, had moved closer to Caleb until she was leaning against him for comfort.

Caleb was ignorant to it until he woke to find her curled against his side with her head resting on his arm. He looked down at the woman that was asleep next to him. He was afraid to move in fear of creating a scene like the previous morning resulting in another head injury. Her dark curls framed her heart shaped face and the long black lashes accented her almond shaped eyes. Her cheeks and the tip of her nose were rosy from the cold air. He'd never seen anyone as beautiful as this stranger that was curled against him. His heart jumped in his chest as the urge to protect her overcame him. The trance was broken when she took a deep breath as she started to wake. Her eyes opened but she didn't move from the comfort by his side. She looked up confused by her surrounding. Her day began with a warm smile.

"Good morning," Caleb managed to whisper. His words had a difficult time passing the lump in his throat. He swallowed hard to try and clear it. "*Caleb Whitworth! What is wrong with you? You're acting like a love sick school boy!"* he scolded himself. She sat up and smiled at him. "Watch your head," he teased.

She let out a welcomed giggle from his comment then realized she was practically sitting in his lap. "Excuse me! I'm so sorry, I must have… the wind…" she was so embarrassed she couldn't look at him.

Caleb laughed but didn't comment. He didn't have any complaints.

They crawled out from under the wagon through mud and wet grass. It was a beautiful morning. There was a light fog lifting from the trees and the birds welcomed the day with singing. The sun was making its appearance causing the wet foliage to sparkle like a million diamonds.

Lauren took in the beauty of the morning and breathed in the crisp air. "Be still, and know that I *am* God: I will be exalted among the heathen, I will be exalted in the earth," she absent mindedly quoted the verse aloud. It was then that she remembered her bible. She ran to the wagon bench and retrieved the wet bundle. As she expected, her bible was ruined. She held it close to her chest and hugged it.

Caleb noticed her sorrow over the ruined book. "I can't understand how you can believe God exists and that He loves you; but yet He can allow you to be in your situation," Caleb grunted.

"It's through the trials that I become strong in my faith. I believe He is with me at all times and He will not give me more than I can bear."

Lauren smiled at him realizing he wasn't a believer of her Lord. He wouldn't understand.

"But, what about your parents' deaths? Did they love Him and worship Him? If so why did He allow them to be killed?" he asked.

"I don't know, Mr. Whitworth. I do know that He has a plan and His plan is perfect. I only see the small picture but know in my heart the big picture's already painted." She saw the doubt in his eyes.

"Lord, help me to show him who you are. He's been so good to me and the best I can give him in return is to show him your gift of salvation," she silently prayed.

"I'll get the horses ready if you'll help with the meal. I doubt we'll find dry wood so we'll have to pass on the coffee," Caleb instructed.

Changing the subject was his way of dropping it all together. His ma claimed to love the Lord and He took her and left his pa to raise four young boys. But there was something about Lauren's conviction that kept him wondering about what she had said. With every passing moment he spent with her the more intrigued he was with her. He knew he needed to get to Jenkins and get there fast.

****

Jenkins' silhouette was a welcomed sight for Lauren. She was chilled to the bone and her body ached from sitting up all night. The last couple of days were draining and all she could think about was a hot meal, warm bed, and a good night's sleep. Lauren panicked when she suddenly realized she had no money to pay for such luxuries.

During the past few days the two travelers grew more comfortable in conversation. When Lauren suddenly grew quiet Caleb sensed the change in her mood.

"Is something wrong? We'll be in Jenkins soon. I thought you'd be excited," he said.

She was looking down and was nervously twirling a stray thread around one of her fingers.

"Lauren?"

She looked in the distance and started to say something but she couldn't get the words out.

Caleb pulled the team. "Lauren, look at me." He turned her and held her so she had to look at him. She raised her eyes to his. "Tell me what's wrong." The tone of his voice was firm but she could tell by the look in his eyes he was concerned.

"I'm a mess; my hair's a mess," she started hysterically, "and this dress! It's caked with mud and ripped!" She grabbed her skirt to show him.

Caleb was so amused by her outburst that he had to turn his head so she couldn't see he was trying to hide his smile. He admired her spunk after all she'd been through.

"…and," she hesitated and drew in a deep breath before continuing in almost a whisper, "I don't have any money."

Her last statement made him sit back and scold himself for not assuring her he'd take care of her needs while he was there.

"Don't worry; I'm not going to dump you in the streets – unless of course you find a more suitable wagon to hide in." He grinned trying to lighten her mood.

Lauren snapped her head up in astonishment from his comment but her anger faded when she saw him smiling and realized he was joking.

"I can't possibly burden you further Mr. Whitworth. You've done so much for me already. I know you probably don't believe this but I know God was watching over me the night I ran away and he'll continue to protect me; so you don't need to worry about me once we get to Jenkins. I've delayed your travel too long and I know you want to get home." She was very sincere.

Caleb knew he should be relieved that she was willing to stay in Jenkins. Wasn't it, a couple days ago he couldn't wait to get there to do just that – leave her? She put so much trust in this God she talked so fondly about. He thought of their conversation earlier that day about her faith. He wondered how she could believe so strongly in someone or *something* they couldn't see. She risked her life trusting she'd be protected by Him. What if his wagon wasn't the only one in the livery that night? Not all men would have cared for her without… he didn't want to think about what could have happened to her. She was a beautiful woman and she took a great risk in what she did. The dangers she put herself in once again gave him that over powering desire to protect her. In his thirty-two years he'd never felt such confusion and frustration.

They rode the rest of the way in silence, both deep in their own thoughts.

Caleb stopped the wagon in front of the town's hotel. Lauren was thankful to finally be able to stretch her tired legs and back. She felt as if the wagon had driven over her. She followed Caleb into the hotel but didn't approach the desk with him. She was so embarrassed by her appearance she kept her back to the clerk and pretended to be interested in the paintings on the wall.

"I'll take two rooms and I'd like a bath sent up for the lady please."

When she heard Caleb order a bath for her she wanted to shout for joy.

Caleb saw the excitement in her face and laughed. "You'd think I ordered you a million dollars! I've never known anyone to get so excited about a bath!"

"Mr. Whitworth, you don't know...." she started but he wouldn't let her continue.

"Shhh, here's your room key. I need to get a few things from the mercantile; providing they're still open. Enjoy your bath."

For the first time Lauren really looked at this man in front of her. She truly believed in her heart that God had sent her an angel and a very handsome one too. He was smiling at her with such warmth in his eyes it made her blush. He was on his way out when he returned to her side.

"Don't open the door except for the maid or me. I'll be back as soon as I can," he warned.

"I doubt I'll have any problems since you are the only one I know in this town. I'll be fine.

Thank you, Mr. Whitworth." As she smiled her blue eyes sparkled with excitement.

He stopped himself from reaching out to push a stray curl from her face. "You're welcome," he managed to get the words out without stammering. He turned and left before she could sense his emotions.

Lauren watched as he left then had to refrain from running up the stairs to her room. The promise of a steamy bath was almost too much for her to bear.

****

Caleb wasn't sure what he was looking for until he saw the hair brushes and chose one that he thought was suitable. He was headed for the counter when a dress that matched the blue of Lauren's eyes caught his attention. It was trimmed with white lace. Little pearl buttons ran down the front of the bodice. He touched the soft fabric and wondered if it would fit Lauren.

"Can I help you with something, sir?" A young woman was standing on the other side of the dress rack.

Caleb noticed she was about the same height as Lauren.

"Would this fit you?"

His question caused her to giggle before answering him. She walked around to stand next to him; very heavy with child. "Maybe at one time but I doubt it would today!" she laughed.

His face turned red with embarrassment.

"I'm sorry, I couldn't resist. My husband tells me all the time I need to think before I open my mouth but to tell you the truth; I wouldn't have as much fun."

"No harm done." Caleb smiled at her.

"Is your wife with you? Maybe she can come in and try it on. We have a room in the back where..."

"No! She's not here, I mean she's here but she's not my..." Caleb felt the heat rising in his face and he felt like crawling under a rock. "I'll take it."

The woman gave an understanding smile. "Is there anything else I can get you?."

"No, that will be all." He handed her the items he carried and followed her to the counter. He watched as she wrapped his purchase. The bell on the door announced another customer. Caleb was looking at the items on display when he over heard the woman's husband talking to the new arrival.

"Can I help you sir? We're almost ready to close for the day."

"I won't keep you long, I'm wondering if you've seen a woman in here today or maybe yesterday? She's about this tall with black hair and blue eyes."

Caleb's heart stopped. He slowly turned to look at the inquiring man.

"No sir but you can ask my wife. I wasn't here most of the day," the owner answered.

Prather noticed Caleb and the woman behind the counter and approached them. "What about you? Have either of you seen anyone matching this description?"

"No sir, I'm sorry," the young lady answered. When Caleb didn't offer any information Prather cleared his throat to get his attention.

"I just arrived in town." Caleb paid the woman behind the counter and gathered his packages. He turned back to Prather before leaving. "Has this woman caused you problems or is she dangerous? Is there a reward if found?" he asked.

Prather pulled himself to his full height and inspected the stranger in front of him. "She left her betrothed in Hadley without word. He is extremely concerned for her safety. We think she might be here. If you know anything I'm sure my employer will be happy to oblige you with a small token of his appreciation. We are staying in a room at the boarding house."

"Betrothed? What the ...?" Caleb's mind was racing. "No, I haven't seen her." Caleb left the store and let the door slam behind him.

She had made a fool out of him with her tales of her parents' deaths and how she was running for her life. His anger grew as he made his way back to the hotel. He wanted answers and he wanted them now!

****

"Will that be all ma'am?" the hotel maid asked Lauren after preparing her bath.

"Yes, thank you very much." She practically pushed the young girl from her room so she could submerge herself in the hot bath water. Small bottles of different scented soaps were on a table next to the tub. Lauren almost ripped the tattered dress from her body before sliding into the hot water. She allowed the warmth to ease the aches of her sore muscles before submerging her head under the scented water. When she was sure her hair was completely saturated she sat up and lathered it and scrubbed hard to remove the dirt from the past few days. Satisfied with the scouring she took a deep breath and went under to rinse out the soap. She didn't hear the door bang against the wall when Caleb kicked it open.

He threw the packages on the bed and looked around for her. He was baffled when he didn't see her. He heard the sound of splashing water then noticed a privacy screen in the corner of the room. He tossed the screen aside knocking the little table and bottles on the floor. He could barely see the tops of her knees above the bubbles. Without hesitating he plunged in the water and grabbed her by an arm.

She sat up stunned. Her wet hair covered her face causing her to cough as she tried to breath.

"Get out!" Caleb's voice was deep with fury.

She managed to push her hair from her face and looked up at him. His face was dark with anger causing her to shrink back against the tub.

"What?" she gasped.

"Get out now!" he yelled trying not to raise his voice any louder.

"I will not! Mr. Whitworth! Please!" she pleaded with him.

He grabbed the towel next to the tub and held it up for her. "Get out now before I drag you out myself." He turned his head to give her some privacy.

Lauren didn't wait to see if he'd follow through with his threat. She quickly stood up and wrapped the towel around her. She stepped out of the tub and stood next to his tall frame. She was shaking from head to toe not from the chill in the room but from Caleb's unexpected fit of anger.

He turned toward Lauren. The rage on his face frightened her so much she couldn't move. "What?" Her eyes were wide with fright. Water dripped off her hair forming small puddles around her feet. "Mr. Whitworth, what did I do?" she whispered.

"It's what you didn't do," he spat.

Lauren searched for a reason why he'd be so angry with her. She had locked the door after he left and had only let the maid in. That's when she looked at him alarmed. "Did I not lock the door? I thought I did after the maid left I'm sorry!" She thought that was the cause of his distress. How else did he get into her room?

Caleb wasn't going to fall for her innocent act any longer. He dragged her to a chair and pushed her in it so hard it slid back. He leaned on the arms and bent so close to her she was forced to look him in the face. "Why don't you start by telling me the truth?" he hissed.

"The truth about what?" she asked.

"About being engaged to Bailey? What? Did you get cold feet? Is that why you ran?" He stood up and backed away so he could read her face.

She jumped to her feet catching Caleb off guard. "What are you talking about? I've never been engaged to anyone! How dare you accuse me of lying to you! Everything I told you is the truth!" She pulled the towel closer around her shoulders. "Who told you such lies?" Her anger now matched his.

"Someone was looking for a woman who matched your description. I ran into him at the mercantile."

Lauren's face turned white and her legs gave out from under her. Caleb caught her before her knees hit the ground and helped her to the chair. "My uncle?" she softly asked.

"No, I've never seen this man before. He's tall and very thin but from what I gathered he works for your uncle – or your *betrothed* as he called him."

"I have to leave." Fear gripped at Lauren. She was no longer concerned about the accusations Caleb threw at her. She grabbed the filthy dress she removed earlier. "I need to get dressed, please leave my room," she ordered.

"No," Caleb answered flatly. "I'm not going anywhere until I get some answers and I want them now!"

"I don't have the answers!" she yelled back. "I don't know why Prather would tell you I was engaged to my uncle. Please leave! I need to get dressed!" She lunged toward Caleb and tried to push him toward the door but it was like trying to move a brick wall. He held her at arms length but she continued to push at him.

"Please, Mr. Whitworth! I have to leave before he finds me!" She gave up on her struggle to move him and surrendered to tears.

Caleb growled and ushered her back to the chair. He set her down this time without causing assault to her back side. He grabbed the foot stool and sat across from her so they were facing each other. "You know this man?" he asked her.

"His name is Alex Prather. My uncle hired him to keep an eye on me." Her tears were flowing freely down her face.

Caleb stood up and paced the room trying to come to some conclusion. He tossed his hat on a table and ran his hand through his dark hair. *"Why would her uncle want to marry her?"*

"Did your father leave you any money?" he asked her.

"Of course! How could I have been so blind?" She jumped up and was the one now pacing the room. "My father had a trust fund for me in the event of his death. I'm not to receive it until I'm twenty-one or..." she stopped in her tracks, "if I get married; whichever comes first." Her uncle's motive was clear to her now. "How could I have been so stupid? He needs me for the money my father left me!" She looked at Caleb. "Please don't let him find me. He's my legal guardian until I'm twenty-one and there is no one who can stop him from legally taking me."

The pleading in her eyes tore at his heart. How could he resist such a request? He needed to get away from her before he gathered her in his arms. He wanted to assure her everything was going to be fine. *"This is insane!"* His thoughts startled him. He grabbed his hat and jammed it on his head.

"I'm going to get us something to eat then we'll figure out what we're going to do. Wedge this chair under the door knob and under *no* circumstances are you to open it until I get back." She stood motionless staring at the floor. "Do you understand?" He had to raise his voice in order to snap her back to the present.

"Yes," she answered feebly.

"Good. I won't be long," he said in a softer tone.

He left the room but didn't make his way down the hall until he heard her secure the door with the chair. He broke the lock when he charged in earlier leaving the chair the only thing between her and any unwanted guests.

Lauren was beside herself after Caleb left. She put her dirty dress on and tried to relax. She'd sit down and within minutes she was back on her feet pacing the room. Did he leave her here to fend for herself? She felt sick to her stomach and her head was pounding. She knelt down on her knees and prayed that the Lord would show her direction and that Caleb didn't leave her. She prayed that her uncle wouldn't discover her and she'd some how get out of town before he knew she was there. Every nerve in her body was frayed. When she heard a soft tap on the door she almost jumped out of her skin. On shaking legs she cautiously approached the door.

"Who is it?" she whispered.

"It's me," Caleb answered.

She let out a sigh of relief when she heard his deep voice and quickly opened the door.

He was holding a tray with sandwiches and fruit he purchased from the hotel diner. Caleb told the owner Lauren wasn't feeling well and asked if they had something he could bring to her. He sat Lauren down at a small table and tried to get her to eat. She tried but was afraid it wouldn't stay down her stomach was so nauseous.

"You look miserable," Caleb told her. "You need to eat something before you get sick."

"Thanks a lot." She glanced at him, embarrassed by her appearance.

He noticed she was wearing her soiled dress and remembered the one he had purchased for her. He brought the brown package to her.

"Here, maybe this will help brighten your spirits a little." He smiled not knowing what else to do for her.

"What is it?" she asked.

"Open it!" He started to pull on the strings that held the brown paper in place.

When she saw the dress she didn't know what to say. She sat looking at it and stroked the soft fabric. "Thank you, Mr. Whitworth, it's beautiful." She finally managed to say. His kindness overwhelmed her and confused her at the same time. One minute he was accusing her of lying and then he was presenting her with a new dress.

"Put it on," he said as he stepped out of the room.

Lauren quickly put the new dress on and smoothed the front of the skirt. It was so soft against her skin. Other then it being a little too long; it fit her perfectly. She went to the door and let Caleb back in the room.

He whistled and smiled at her beauty. Her long black hair hung loose past her hips. The fabric's blue made the color of her eyes shine. "Well now, that looks much better. Oh, yeah, here. I got this for you too. I thought you might need it." He went to the bed and found the hair brush and handed it to her.

She smiled at his kind act. She sat in front of the small fireplace and tried to brush her hair. It was so tangled from neglect that she had to stop to rest her arm.

Caleb watched as he ate and noticed how tired she looked. He brought the foot stool and placed it in front of her.

"Sit here." He pointed to the stool. She did as he told her and was shocked when he sat in the chair directly behind her. "Let me have the brush."

She handed it to him and allowed him to brush out the tangles. He started at the bottom and gently worked his way up until her hair was tangle free and shining in the firelight.

She sat with her eyes closed and was actually able to relax while he tended to her hair. She almost forgot her dilemma until he spoke.

"Lauren, when do you turn twenty-one?"

"December."

"Six months from now," he though out loud. "I think I might have a solution to your situation."

Lauren opened her eyes and turned to face him to see if he was serious. She searched his face and it was clear he had been doing some thinking.

"What?" The look of hope on her face melted

Caleb's heart.

"Marry me," he said without hesitation.

Lauren stared at him in disbelief. The words played over in her head.

"Marry me, marry me...."

"Lauren?" Caleb put his hand on her shoulder. "Did you hear me?"

"Marry you?" She jumped to her feet and looked at him in astonishment. "Marry you? Mr. Whitworth, have you lost your mind? How in the world is that going to help me?" She turned her back to him and looked up at the ceiling not believing what she just heard.

"That went well, now what do I do?" Caleb asked himself. He turned her to face him before he continued.

"Just hear me out. It wouldn't be like a marriage – marriage; it would be more like ... a written agreement. We'd be married on paper for six months only, then after you turn twenty-one we'll have it annulled. Bailey wouldn't be able to touch you." He stopped to see her reaction.

"I will be marked as a loose woman after the annulment. I don't think so," she hissed.

"No one would have to know that we were married," he explained further.

She thought about his proposal and wondered if it would actually work. "I'd go home with you?" she asked.

"Yes. You'd be welcomed there. All my family needs to know is that you needed a place to stay until you could go back to your home in Cape Jennings." He noticed that she had calmed down after the initial shock of his proposal.

"What reason will we give them as to why I can't go home?" She wanted to know every detail of his plan.

"I haven't thought that far ahead yet. All I know is that Bailey is here now and if he discovers you are too, I can't stop him from taking you. We need to do something today and we'll work on the rest later."

Lauren was quiet for a moment while she weighed her options. "Paper only?" she asked with a skeptical look.

"Yes," he answered with a laugh. He knew what was on her mind. "I promise to keep my distance."

"It's a deal," she said.

They shook hands to seal the contract.

Chapter Seven

"Do you Caleb Allen Whitworth; take Lauren Elizabeth Bailey to be your lawfully wedded wife?"

"I do."

"Do you Lauren Elizabeth Bailey; take Caleb Allen Whitworth to be your lawfully wedded husband"

"Do I?" Lauren stood there frozen. She felt Caleb give her hand a little squeeze.

"It'll be ok, I promise," he whispered in her ear.

"I do," she finally answered.

The rest of the ceremony was a blur as she tried to sort out her emotions.

"You may kiss the bride," the preacher announced.

Caleb lifted her face and placed a tender kiss on her mouth. He held her eyes with his for what seemed an eternity while he softly stroked the side of her face with his thumb. Paper only he reminded himself and was sorry for doing so. She was legally his but he made an agreement with her and he would stick to his word.

"Congratulations!" the hotel owner said. He and his wife witnessed their wedding for them. The older man slapped Caleb on the back and shook his hand. He pulled him away from Lauren and his wife so he could speak to him privately. "She's very beautiful. She fits the description of a woman someone is looking for. I thought I'd warn you to take care when leaving in the morning young man. Watch your back."

"Thank you, sir, I will and I'm sorry about the door. I'll pay to have it repaired and if it's okay with you I'll move our stuff in the other room for the night." Caleb could only imagine what was going through the man's head.

They continued to speak about Caleb's plans for the morning while the women softly chattered back and forth.

When Caleb and Lauren had the room to themselves they gathered the few belongings and relocated to the room across the hall. The fire was lit and cast a warm glow in the room. Lauren was exhausted and the bed was very inviting.

"I'm going to see to the team. I'll be back soon. Don't....."

"...open the door to anyone but you," she finished his sentence for him.

"Very submissive, good wife," he teased.

Lauren just rolled her eyes at him but had no energy to retaliate as he left the room. She undressed and slid between the sheets. She was so tired but the events of the day kept running through her mind. Did she do the right thing? Was she trusting God for answers or running on her own?

She remembered the story of Abraham and Sara and how he lied to King Abimelech. He told him that Sarah was his sister and not his wife. Abraham was afraid that the king would kill him so he could have Sarah. Abraham didn't trust God to keep him safe so God visited Abimelech in a dream and warned him not to touch Sarah because she was another man's wife or he would be a dead man.

She thought about Caleb and wondered if marrying him would bring him danger or worse yet; if it would interfere in a chance to tell him about Jesus and His sovereign love.

She tried to get warm but the chills ran through her like ice water. She snuggled deep under the blankets and tried to fall asleep. She heard Caleb enter the room but didn't let him know she was still awake. He moved around the room quietly so he wouldn't wake her. He settled for the night on the floor next to the fire. Soon she heard his even breathing and knew he was asleep.

The thought of a man committing the next six months of marriage to her in order to keep her safe softened her heart. She lifted Caleb up to the Lord and thanked Him for the man who appointed himself as her guardian. She tried to find sleep but her mind wouldn't let her rest as she thought about what the next several months had in store for her.

She didn't know when or how long she had been sleeping when Caleb tried to wake her the next morning.

"Lauren, come on we need to get moving." Caleb gently shook her shoulder.

She didn't want to move from the comfort of the blankets. She received very little sleep and wanted to just lay there and forget about everything. Her entire body ached and chills ran through her.

"I had breakfast brought up. You need to eat something before we head out. You've barely eaten enough in the past few days to feed a bird."

Lauren forced her tired body to sit up. "Could you please turn around so I can get dressed?" she asked still half asleep.

Caleb did as she asked and waited for her to approach the table before he joined her. Her face was flushed and there were dark circles under her eyes.

"Are you feeling ok? You look awful," he said.

"You know, you're going to have to work on your compliments. Yesterday you told me I looked miserable and today I look awful. I'm beginning to think marriage is not agreeing with me."

Caleb let out a hearty laugh. It amazed him she could have a sense of humor in her situation. "I'm sorry. I know this has been rough on you. By this time tomorrow we'll be at Eden and you can catch up on your rest and Annie will put some meat on your bones." He was in a good mood. Lauren liked it when he smiled.

She surveyed the feast before her; bread, cheese, jams, bacon, and hard boiled eggs. As good as it looked her stomach warned her not to eat too much. She then noticed a small china tea pot. "Oh, how wonderful! I haven't had tea in so long." She poured herself some of the steamy liquid and sat with both hands around the tiny cup. She closed her eyes and breathed in the aroma of the warm drink.

"You're so easy to please." Caleb smiled at her. "I do wish you'd eat something though." He handed her a plate.

She took a piece of bread and some bacon and nibbled on it. Even though it was the end of June and warm outside she couldn't shake the chills. She knew she was getting sick but didn't want to alarm Caleb. He was so excited about getting home she didn't want to worry him or cause him further delays.

"Do you think the hotel owners would mind if I wrapped up what we don't eat?" she asked.

"I don't see why not since I paid for it." He got up from the table and grabbed his hat. "I'm going to bring the team around back. I'll be back shortly."

"It'll be ready when you return," she assured him.

"Good, lock the door," he instructed before he left the room.

She felt like a fool asking about the food. Of course he had paid for it. She didn't know what she was thinking but her question didn't seem to bother him.

She gathered their few belongings and had them ready in no time. She waited patiently for Caleb while looking out the window. It was going to be a pretty day. The sun was just lighting the sky and there wasn't a cloud to be seen. She walked away from the window and tried to relax. Her body still ached and she was feeling light headed so she sat down. She closed her eyes and started to fall asleep when Caleb returned for her. She gathered what strength she could find to stand and help him carry everything to the wagon. The hotel owner and his wife were there waiting for them.

"Here." The owner's wife handed Lauren a small package. "I didn't have time to get this ready for you yesterday. It's not much but I felt I needed to give it to you."

Lauren opened the tiny box and pulled out a silver hair comb. "It's beautiful!" Lauren whispered. "You didn't need to do this." She hugged the older woman.

"No, I didn't, but I wanted to. You didn't have family or such here. You looked so alone and scared out of your mind! He seems to be a good man."

"He is," Lauren said as she watched Caleb and the hotel owner check the team and wagon.

They bid their farewells and were on their way.

"Who's Annie?" Lauren asked. She had so many questions.

"She's our housekeeper. You'll like her," he answered her.

"Is Eden big?"

Caleb liked that she was interested and decided to fill her in on his family and what she should expect. "You might say that. It's one of the bigger ranches in the area. My parents worked hard to get it going and it's paid off. My ma used to call it her Little Garden Of Eden, so my pa named it Eden."

"She must have liked that." Lauren was trying to stay focused on the conversation and not on how horrible she felt.

"She did. My parents were inseparable. She'd ride the range with pa often until I came along and then she was happy taking care of Jake and me."

"Jake is your brother I assume?"

"Yup, one of three. Ma died when the twins were born, that's when pa hired Annie." He had a far away look in his eyes.

"I'm sorry, Mr. Whitworth. I didn't mean to bring up sad memories."

"Don't be, and its Caleb. There are no formalities at Eden so it would be nice if you called me Caleb. Not only that, there are five Mr. Whitworth's and it will be less confusing." He was teasing her again and it made her feel at ease.

They talked about Caleb's brothers and the ranch and the upcoming Independence Day picnic. She smiled at his excitement and knew that he couldn't wait to get to his much loved Eden.

The June sun was high overhead and warm on Lauren's back but did little to warm her inside. The chills were constant and as hard as she tried to get warm she couldn't.

"Mr.....Caleb, can we stop for a minute? I need to see to some needs." She hated to delay his progress but she really needed to get out of the wagon. She felt like her stomach was going to empty right where she sat.

Caleb saw her flushed cheeks and wished she wouldn't be so embarrassed when she was around him.

"Good idea. I'm getting hungry." He looked up at the sun. "Looks to be around lunch time anyway."

Lauren didn't pay much attention to the gradual change in scenery from the flat planes to the rolling foothills and thicker patches of trees. Her head ached. She tried to shield her eyes from the bright sun. She was relieved when Caleb picked a shady area to rest the team. She jumped from the wagon before Caleb could help her and stumbled when her weak legs almost gave out from under her. Caleb was busy with the horses and didn't notice her near tumble. She walked quickly to a patch of thick brush and sat down to catch her breath. She tried to still the queasiness she felt. When she returned to the wagon she scolded herself. Caleb already had the lunch spread out on a cloth. She sat down and tried to eat listening to Caleb describe more of his home to her. She managed a weak smile now and then to assure him she was listening.

Caleb noticed her quiet mood but dismissed it thinking she was getting nervous about meeting his family.

"We're making good time. The horses know we are headed for home and they're just as excited to get there." Still no comment from Lauren. "Are you scared to meet them?"

"Your family?" Lauren asked surprised.

"Yeah, you've been pretty quiet. I thought you might be thinking twice about staying at Eden." For some reason this really bothered Caleb but he didn't know why.

"No, I'm fine. Is there a telegraph office in - what did you say the name of the town was?" she asked.

"Clayton's Creek. There is but I don't know if the lines are repaired. I tried to wire pa from Jenkins to let him know I was okay. The storm knocked them out. I guess you'll need to let all your beaus back home know you're okay." He didn't lift his head from his meal but carefully glanced in her direction to catch her reaction. He wondered who she needed to wire.

She didn't look up nor flinch at his teasing. "No, I need to contact my father's lawyer to see what kind of money I have. I need to know my financial state for later," she explained.

"Let's get going. I think the horses rested long enough." He stood up and gave his hand to Lauren to help her. As soon as she tried to stand she crumpled in a pile at his feet.

"Lauren?" He knelt next to her and turned her so he could see her face. She was hot to his touch. He cradled her head in his arm and gently tapped her face with his free hand. "Lauren! Come on girl - wake up!"

He retrieved a canteen from the wagon and splashed cool water on her face. She moaned but didn't open her eyes. He had to get help. He made a comfortable place for her in the back of the wagon. He covered her with what he could find to keep her warm. She shivered uncontrollably. He pushed the horses as hard as he dared. Sensing his urgency and their want to get home Caleb had to pull back on the reins with all the strength he had to keep them from running themselves to death.

He stopped often to check her condition delaying his return home. When it became too dark and he could no longer drive the team safely he stopped for the night. He made a fire and piled pine needles and leaves for a bed for Lauren. He quickly tended to the horses and ran back to her side. Her hair was plastered around her face from sweat. He held the canteen to her mouth to try to get her to drink.

"No mamma! No don't drink it!" She shoved the canteen away from her mouth.

"Lauren - it's Caleb. You need to drink some water."

He tried again to get her to drink but she fought against it. She moaned and cried in her unconscious state until Caleb no longer knew what to do. He never felt so helpless in his life. He held her in his arms and wept.

"God," he whispered, "I know I don't ever talk to you but I need you to please help her. Not for me but for her. She has so much faith and trust in you. Please help her. She never turned her back on you through all her troubles."

He wasn't sure if his prayer would be heard but it gave him a sense of peace as he held her in his arms and softly spoke to her through the night.

****

"Afternoon Mr. Whitworth. I still don't have a wire from Caleb." Nate hated to give Will the bad news. He knew Caleb should already be home and how much Will's been worried about him. "I've been informed that the lines will be up sometime today – no later than tomorrow morning and as soon as they are I'll send a wire to Jenkins to see if they've seen him."

"Thanks Nate, I'd appreciate that." Will headed toward the sheriff's office. He was deep in thought and didn't see the pretty blonde and accidentally bumped into her.

"Excuse me, Miss Cynthia! I didn't see you!" he said as he removed his hat.

"Why Mr. Whitworth, it's a wonder you saw me at all. You look like you're a thousand miles away." Her voice was as smooth as silk. "Where on earth is that son of yours? I thought he'd be back by now." She stood close not allowing him to pass by. "You don't think he's found someone and ran away, do you?" she said laughing.

"I highly doubt that. Don't you worry yourself about Caleb, he'll be home soon. I've been told there was some bad weather and I'm sure that's what's causing his delay. Now, if you'll excuse me." He replaced his hat on his head and gave her a polite nod as he tried to continue on his way.

Cynthia Redding had been chasing Caleb for as long as Will could remember. Caleb was always polite but that's as far as he'd take it. He was careful not to give her any false hopes or the wrong impression, but this never seemed to discourage her.

"Please tell him I was asking about him," she said as she smiled sweetly.

"Yes'm, I will." Will finally managed to slip away from Cynthia and make it to Tim's office.

He walked in as Tim was trying his best to calm Mrs. Hampton's anger.

"I'm telling you sheriff, if you don't keep them boys out of my yard I will take matters into my own hands!" Mrs. Hampton yelled.

There was no doubt in Will's mind that she was complaining about a few boys eating her apples from her trees again.

"No need for that Mrs. Hampton, I'll see their parents at church Sunday and I'll make sure to bring it up. In the meantime, I'd advise you to let me handle it." He tried to be as courteous as he could to the old woman as he ushered her out the door. Will allowed his laughter to fill the room after the door closed behind the mumbling woman.

"For goodness sakes, you'd think she could spare a few apples," Tim said between chuckles. He poured coffee for them before he sat down at his desk. "You heard from Caleb yet?"

"No, I'm thinking about heading toward Jenkins tomorrow afternoon if he's not home by then." He took a sip of coffee before continuing. "If the wagon broke down he'd leave it and head on in without it. I just can't figure what's keeping the boy."

"Let me know if you want me to ride with you. I can use some time away from here," Tim volunteered.

Clayton's Creek was a quiet town and would be fine for one day without the sheriff. He did leave someone in the office for major problems - like apple thieves and the occasional Friday night drunks.

"I sure will. I'll send word with Jake. He's coming in tonight to eat at Sally Ann's," Will said with a wink.

"Un, hun." Tim smiled as he leaned his chair back on two legs. "Do you think we'll ever hear wedding bells with those boys of yours? Every girl in town would like to hook one of them."

"They're too serious about the ranch. I think Ev or Ethan will marry before Caleb or Jake." He answered as he got up to leave. "Well Tim, I'm going back to Eden. Bring your wife out for dinner sometime. Annie would sure like some womanly company."

"Thanks, we'll do that. You take care now."

Will's decision to look for Caleb calmed his nerves a bit. He left Tim's office feeling better until he saw that Cynthia Redding was headed toward him again. He quickly turned in the other direction before she noticed him. Though he knew she was after Caleb she had a way of making him feel very uncomfortable whenever she was around him. He waited until the coast was clear before he continued on his way home.

Will joined his sons at the breakfast table the next morning dreading the thought of having to look for him. His hopes that Caleb would return home the previous day were crushed.

"If Caleb's not home by this afternoon, Tim and I are going to head for Jenkins. I'll need you to see to things here while I'm gone." Will instructed Jake while they ate breakfast.

"Do you think something happened?" Evan asked between bites.

"I hope not but I can't wait around here any longer," Will answered.

"Pa, can I go with you?" Ethan asked with hope in his eyes.

"No, I need you and Ev to haul the hay to the loft. Nate assured me the wire lines should be fixed today. I'll send word from Jenkins to let you know if I found him."

Will wiped his mouth and got up from the table. He went to the gun cabinet and picked out a rifle and pistol. The boys exchanged concerned glances as they left for the barn.

"Ethan misses Caleb when he's gone, you should let him go with you," Jake suggested.

"No, he needs to work here and get his head out of books," Will answered without looking at Jake.

"Why don't you let Ethan continue his education like you did Caleb? He's smart and he's wasting time hauling hay and branding cattle." Jake knew how much Ethan wanted to go to school to study medicine but Will thought it was a waste of time; after all, he did very well without all the books and schooling.

"Caleb's education was your ma's idea; not mine. He's just going through a stage, he'll get over it."

Jake wasn't about to let the matter drop but Ethan burst in the door.

"Pa! Come quick! It's Caleb, he's home but something's wrong, he's running the team hard!"

Ethan ran back outside with Jake and Will close behind him. They heard Caleb shouting at the team as he urged them toward the barn.

"Whoa!" He pulled on the reigns to stop the thundering team.

The horses' nostrils flared from the heavy breathing and their bodies were lathered from the rapid pace. Will grabbed hold of one of the bridles to inspect the horse.

"Have you gone mad son?" he shouted at his oldest but Caleb didn't hear him as he jumped down and ran to the back of the wagon.

"I need doc out here now!" he shouted. He

lifted a small form in his arms. "Annie!" he shouted at the top of his lungs.

Annie ran out of the house when she heard the urgency in his voice. "What is it lad?" She met him half way and saw what she thought was a child in his arms. "My word Caleb, what do you have there?"

He didn't stop to answer her as he carried Lauren to the house.

"Put her in the guest room," Annie instructed as she followed him as fast she could.

"No." Caleb took the stairs two at a time and gently placed her on his bed.

It was then that Annie saw it was a young woman and not a child. She looked at the flushed face of the stranger he had brought into the house. "She's burn'n with fever. We need to get her cooled down. How long has she been sick?" Annie asked as she felt Lauren's head.

"Yesterday - I think. She's looked tired for a few days but I didn't pay any attention to it. I thought she just needed sleep but yesterday when we stopped for lunch she fainted. I've not been able to wake her." He stood helpless next to the bed and allowed Annie to take charge.

"Evan, fetch the doctor, Ethan, bring up the tub and fill it with cool water. There's a jug of vinegar in the pantry. Bring that too. I'll need you all to leave the room so I can remove her clothes." Annie issued orders to the dumbfounded men standing around. Lauren let out a weak moan. "Now, now lass, I'm here to take care of ya," Annie assured her.

Caleb was frozen where he stood.

"Annie'll take care of her, come on, there's nothing you can do now." Jake pulled Caleb by the arm trying to convince his older brother she was in good hands.

"No, I'm not leaving her until I know she'll be alright." Caleb pulled his arm from Jake's grip.

Jake knew better then to argue with him when he had his mind set.

Ethan entered the room with the tub and vinegar. Jake, Ethan, and Will ran back and forth with pails of water until the tub was full. When Annie was satisfied there was enough she added the vinegar. "This should help with the fever. Now, everyone shoo." She pushed them out and closed the door. She started to undress Lauren when she realized Caleb was still in the room. He stood looking down at the tiny woman on the bed. "If you're going to stay help me get her in the tub," she told him.

They stripped her down to her chemise. Caleb gently lifted her from the bed. Annie watched while he slowly lowered her in the cool water and spoke to her in a hushed tone. His face was tender as he held her with one arm and sprinkled the water over her shoulders. They bathed her until the water brought her temperature down. Caleb pulled her from the tub and wrapped her in a blanket. When all but her hair and chemise were dry Annie insisted he leave the room until she put a clean night shirt on her. He paced the hall outside of his room until Annie opened the door to let him back in. Lauren was lost in the big bed with piles of blankets around her.

"Not much more to be done till the doctor gets

here," Annie told Caleb. "We just need to keep her warm. Who is she?"

"I met her in Hadley; she needed a place to stay for awhile." That was all the information he gave her. She wondered if there was more then what he was telling her.

"Will she be alright?" he asked Annie with pleading eyes.

"The doctor will be here soon and he'll let us know. Caleb, you'll do the lass no good if you don't get some rest yourself. I'll look after her." She tried to get him to leave.

"No, she might wake up and she'll be scared. I need to stay." He wasn't going to budge.

"Very well then, I'll make some broth. We need to get some nourishment and fluids in her. See if you can get her to drink some water while I'm gone."

Annie walked into the family room to be greeted with a thousand questions all at once. Who is she? Why is she here? What happened? How did they meet?

"I only know they met in Hadley and she needed a place to stay. That's all he'd tell me."

It was late in the evening before Evan returned from town without the doctor. "Doc wasn't there. Miss Laurie down the creek is having her baby. I'm sorry, Pa," he said while trying to catch his breath.

"You did all you could." He put his arm around Evan's shoulders for reassurance. "I'll let Annie know."

He quietly entered the bedroom and watched as Annie and Caleb tried to get Lauren to drink the broth but she wasn't cooperating. Her fever worsened and she moaned in her discomfort. He listened as Caleb softly spoke to her and Annie swabbed her brow with a cool cloth. Annie noticed Will standing in the door.

"Is the doctor here?" she questioned.

Caleb shot a look of relief at his father then panicked when he shook his head.

"He's with Miss Laurie. It's her time but Evan left word. I'm sure he'll be here as soon as he can." He tried to sound positive for his son's sake.

"That could take hours," Caleb grumbled under his breath. He returned his attention to Lauren.

Will went back downstairs. "The fever is worse. All we can do is try to keep her comfortable until doc gets here. You all need to get to work, no sense sitting around here worrying. That's not going to help with anything," he told them. Ethan pushed past his brothers and went out the door. "Ethan!" Will shouted but he ran off toward the creek.

"Let him go pa, I'll help Ev with the hay," Jake told him as he and Evan went out the door.

****

Ethan found what he was looking for near the creek and gathered what he needed. When he returned to the house he brewed a dark tea from willow bark and brought it to his brother. He admired Caleb and looked up to him. He wanted to help if he could. He handed the steaming brew to his older brother.

"What is it?" Caleb asked while he smelled the unusual aroma.

"Willow bark tea. I read in a book that the Indians used it for fevers. I didn't think it would hurt to try." He stood looking at the stranger in his brother's bed.

Caleb smiled at him. "Thanks. At this point we'll try anything. Annie's getting fresh water. You need to help me. I'll sit her up and you try to get her to drink it." He supported Lauren as Ethan put the cup to her lips. She resisted at first but Ethan managed to get her to swallow some of the dark liquid.

"She's very pretty," Ethan remarked. "What's her name?"

Ethan was the only one who thought to ask her name. He had a tender heart and a special gift of caring. Caleb recognized this in his brother and often got angry with his pa when he tried to make him something he'd never be.

"Lauren," Caleb answered, "Lauren Bailey."

"That's a pretty name, it suits her." Ethan felt a little uncomfortable not knowing how she and her brother were acquainted. "I better help with the hay and unload the wagon. I'll make more tea later. I hope it works."

Annie bustled in the room with fresh water as Ethan was leaving. She wrinkled her nose in disgust. "What in heaven's name is that smell?" she asked.

"Willow bark tea. Ethan brought it for Lauren. He read about it in a book and thought it might help with the fever."

"Ah, he's a good lad that one is." She smiled thinking about Ethan's kind action. "Lauren is it? Miss Lauren, I'll leave you with Caleb. I have hungry boys downstairs."

As time passed Caleb noticed that Lauren was sleeping better.

"I'll be darn, its working!" He thought to himself. He managed to get her to drink more tea and by evening her fever broke and she slept quietly. He felt comfortable leaving Lauren's care completely to Annie and sought out one of the guest bedrooms.

Annie reported the good news to the rest of the family when they came in for the night.

Will decided it was time for some answers and went to find Caleb. He checked the room where Lauren was but he wasn't there. He looked in the guest rooms one at a time until he found Caleb on his back sound asleep. He was fully dressed and his boots still on his feet. He closed the door hoping not to wake him. What he needed to know would have to wait till morning.

Chapter Eight

Caleb woke to the sound of someone chopping wood in the yard. He lay on his back for a moment trying to figure out why he was in the guest room when the events of the previous day came flooding back. He jumped out of bed and ran to his bedroom. Annie was coming out just as he got to the door. She saw the concern on his face and didn't hesitate to update him on Lauren's progress.

"Ah, she's doing fine. No fever since last night. The doctor was here this morning and said that Ethan's home-made remedy did the trick. Smart lad he is."

Caleb let out a sigh of relief and hugged Annie. "Thank you Annie." He went for the door but she was quick to stop him.

"You let her rest now. You'll have plenty of time to visit when she's fully aware of her surrounding."

"What do you mean? Did she wake up?" he asked.

"She's out of the woods but she has a long road ahead of her. She's opened her eyes but just for a second or two. She was a little confused about her surroundings but, she'll be fine, you'll see. She just needs rest and good food. Now you better go see your pa. He's been in and out all morning waiting for you to wake up." She stood firm in front of the door to make sure he didn't disturb Lauren.

"My clothes are in there," he challenged her.

"I'll get them," she said still standing in his way. "Get washed and shaved and I'll bring you a fresh change."

He hated to admit it but he was no match for this stubborn, Irish woman. He learned that long ago.

Caleb felt revived after shaving and changing clothes. He was ready to meet his father and didn't have to wait long. Will was seated at his desk with his nose in Eden paperwork when Caleb went downstairs.

Will put his pencil down and leaned back in his chair. "Seems to me you have a lot of explaining to do." He eyed his older son. "Annie left a plate and coffee for you. Get something to eat and come back in here when you're done."

"Yes sir." Caleb knew better then to argue and did what he was told. He ate alone at the kitchen table then returned to Will's office.

"Pa, I'm sorry that I worried you but...." Caleb didn't have a chance to finish before Will interrupted.

"Sit down, son." Will waited for him to be seated before continuing. "Who is she and how do you know her?"

This is the moment that Lauren asked him about in the hotel room. *What are we going to tell your family?* He thought back on her question and decided the truth was best - most of the truth.

"Her name is Lauren Bailey and I met her outside of Hadley. She needed a place to stay until she could return to her home in Cape Jennings to take over her family's business. Both her parents are dead and there's this matter of a greedy uncle who has custody of her until she is twenty one. He was trying to use her to get to her inheritance."

Will leaned forward and glared at his son. "You mean to tell me that; that young lady upstairs is a *runaway*?" he asked.

"No pa, it's not like that! She was in fear for her life! She doesn't have proof but she believes her uncle killed her parents and he was going to kill her next to get the family business and the money."

Will jumped up from his seat and paced the floor behind his desk. "Unbelievable! All this pretty little tart had to do is bat her eyes at you and fill your head with - with lies and you fell for it? For this you had me worried that you were hurt or that one of the horses were down or......Caleb! What were you thinking bringing her here? How do you know she's not in a scheme with her uncle?"

Caleb had never seen his pa so angry. It hurt him to think he didn't trust his judgment. He jumped to his feet in Lauren's defense.

"I told her she'd be welcomed here for as long as she needed to stay and that we never turned anyone in need away from Eden. I guess I was wrong." He stormed out of the house slamming the door behind him.

Will followed him from the office He noticed Annie on the landing and knew she had witnessed the whole thing. "Don't start with me woman," he barked.

"I don't plan to." She started for the kitchen

then turned back to Will. "But you are wrong. He's not a child, Will. You need to give him a little more credit and trust his decisions."

Will plopped down in his seat and let out an angry growl. He thought about the information Caleb had given him. He'd just do some investigating himself. He was determined to get to the bottom of her lies and prove to his son that he couldn't let his feeling get in the way of good judgment. Someday he'd be in charge of Eden and Will didn't want him to lose it to some sweet talking swindler.

****

Lauren heard someone humming. Her eyelids were so heavy she couldn't open her eyes. She focused on the soft tune and couldn't determine if she was really hearing it or if she was dreaming. She willed herself to open her heavy eye lids and drag herself out of the deep slumber she'd been in for the past few days. She felt light headed but the chills and aches were now behind her. She turned toward the humming and saw an older woman in a chair working on her sewing.

"Well there ya be lass!" Her smile was warm. "You gave us a scare that you did, but thanks to our Ethan's quick think'n you came back to us."

Lauren tried to say something but her throat was dry. She ran her tongue across her cracked lips and tried to speak again. "Am I at Eden?" Lauren whispered.

Annie thought her imploring eyes were so big and full of doubt. She looked frightened. "Aye lass, you are for near a week now." Annie got up and poured Lauren a glass of water.

"A week!" Lauren couldn't believe she'd been sick for so long. She tried to sit up in the bed.

"Easy now, you're not ready for dancing just yet! Let me help you." Annie arranged the pillows behind Lauren to give her support. She gladly took the glass of water Annie offered her. It was sweet and the cool temperature soothed her dry throat.

"Do you think you can manage to eat something?" Annie asked.

"I'm not sure." Lauren studied this woman who was sitting on the bed next to her. "You must be Annie."

"Why yes, I am! What did that rascal Caleb have to report about me? Nothing good I'm sure of that," Annie teased.

Lauren liked her jolly manner immediately and began to feel at ease. "He is very fond of you but I'm sure I wasn't supposed to tell you that," Lauren said smiling.

"Well if he wants to eat here, he better show me a wee bit 'o respect. I'll go get you some broth and tea and we'll see how that settles, then we'll go from there." She hesitated before leaving. Her curiosity got the best of her as she remembered how attentive Caleb was to this beautiful woman. She had been wondering what had transpired between the two of them on their way home. She knew she shouldn't pry but she couldn't help it. "Lauren, how is it that you know me Caleb?" Annie watched Lauren's face for any signs that would help her with her curiosity.

Lauren panicked not knowing what Caleb told his family. "*Stay calm,*" she told herself.

"I needed a place to stay for awhile and he told me I could come here. If I'm going to be in the way I'll find other arrangements. Please don't be mad at him. He just wanted to help me."

"No! You'll be fine dear, I was just curious. He didn't share much with me that's all. You are welcomed for as long you need to stay."

Annie watched as Lauren let out a sigh of relief, close her eyes and lay back on the pillow. She knew that there was more between the two of them but, she'd have to be patient and hope that Will was wrong about her.

Chapter Nine

Caleb stayed away from the house since the argument with his pa. He knew Lauren was in good hands with Annie. He would check on her when he returned from the range. He needed time to think about the marriage, his pa's accusations against Lauren, and how he was going to handle the next few months with her staying with them. He had never fought with his pa before and he felt guilty for not telling him the truth. Maybe he underestimated him and he'd understand if he told him everything, but it was too late now. He would just go with the original plan and by the New Year Lauren would be back in Cape Jennings.

He thought about Lauren leaving and sadness crept through him. He pictured her smile and how she blushed so easily one minute then very outspoken the next. He laughed and rubbed his hand over his shin where she had kicked him. She was a fighter all right. His memories were interrupted when Evan sat beside him and poured himself some coffee.

"I'm heading to the house tonight, how about you?" he asked Caleb.

"I think I will too, I've avoided pa long enough."

"Caleb, if you saw how worried he was when you didn't show on time maybe you'd understand why he was so angry." Evan told him.

Caleb thought about his brother's comment and knew he was right but that didn't excuse him from attacking Lauren before he even met her. "You're right, let's see if I can iron things out with him. Let's go home now. Why wait till this evening?"

"Sounds good to me," Evan agreed.

They doused the fire with the leftover coffee and headed home.

****

Annie helped Lauren to a rocking chair on the front porch. She was in need of some good fresh air. She regained most of her strength but was still a little unsteady. The little bit of Eden she could see was breathtaking. Snow capped mountains touched the sky in the distance and the smell of pine was thick in the air.

Lauren was snapping beans Annie had given her when Caleb and Evan rode up to the house. Caleb looked down at her with a big smile on his face.

"It's good to see you up – how ya feeling?" His smiled melted her heart; she didn't realize how much she had missed his company.

"I'm feeling a lot better thanks to Annie. She's been wonderful." Her blue eyes sparkled as she smiled.

Evan let out a whistle. "You better watch out Caleb or someone's gonna snatch her up! On second thought, I think I'll do the snatching!" Evan dismounted and bowed in front of

Lauren. "Evan Whitworth at your service m' lady."

Lauren laughed out loud at his silly action. Caleb snuck up behind him and kicked his backside sending him flying.

"Caleb!" she cried while still laughing. "That was mean!"

Caleb smiled at her. He liked the sound of her using his first name.

"Not to worry, m'lady. I will challenge him to a duel to protect your honor." Evan stood up and used his hat to wipe the dust from his pants and started to laugh. "I'm not kidding brother..."

Caleb quickly interrupted. He didn't need Evan embarrassing him further. "See to the horses before I toss you in the water trough."

Evan laughed and winked at Lauren. He led the horses toward the barn singing.

Caleb sat on a step twirling his hat by its rim while Lauren continued snapping beans. The growing silence made them uncomfortable until Lauren spoke up.

"Annie asked me how we met." She tried to steady her shaking hands while snapping the beans. His presence made her nervous but she didn't' know why. She spent a week with him and never felt this way.

"What did you tell her?" Caleb was hoping to be there when she woke up so they could discuss this further. The argument with his pa ended that.

"I just told her I needed a place to stay for awhile and you offered your home." She was looking at him now with anxiety on her face. "I feel like I'm betraying your family's trust. I don't know how long I can do this."

"Don't feel that way. I told Pa about your uncle and your suspicions about your parents. I told him about the inheritance and that he was after it so you are not hiding anything. It's the truth without all the details. You're not betraying anyone." He made it sound so simple. "Did you meet my pa yet?"

"No, he's been in town with one of your brothers, with the exception of Evan; Annie's the only one I've met."

It was at that moment Annie came out on the porch. She was surprised to see Caleb. "So you've decided to come home have you? You've left this poor dear to fend for herself leaving her like that. You ought to be ashamed of yourself." She ran her hand lovingly over Lauren's head.

"Annie, I know she was in very good care with you here." He stood up to stretch. "What's pa doing in town?"

"I don't know lad, he left with Ethan. He's not been himself since the two of you…" Annie halted her tongue. She didn't want Lauren to know about the argument.

Lauren knew she was hiding something from her. "You had an argument over me being here didn't you?" she asked Caleb.

From the look on her face he knew that only the truth was going to please her. "Yes, but…." he started to explain but Annie interrupted him. "…it'll be alright lass, you wait and see. He was worried about Caleb that's all. Now let's see how those beans look."

Lauren didn't take her eyes off Caleb when she stood and handed Annie the bowl. Without a word, she went in the house and to her room. He assured her she'd be welcomed but she brought arguing in stead.

"Lord, forgive me for not trusting you and following your path. I'm afraid I've brought trouble to this home. Please intervene between father and son and help me to find somewhere else to go." Lauren sat on her bed contemplating on what to do when she heard a soft tap on her door. "Come in."

Annie cracked the door and found Lauren sitting on the edge of her bed looking out the window. She sat next to her and put her arm around her shoulders. The tender action made Lauren miss her mother. As hard as she tried to keep her tears in check they flowed down her cheeks.

"I've made such a mess of things. I didn't want to cause trouble for Caleb and his family." She wiped her tears on the back of her hand.

Annie rocked her back and forth pushing stray curls from her face. "Now, now lass. Don't fret so. It'll be fine you'll see. Mr. Whitworth will see that you're not a threat."

Lauren pulled away from her; shocked by her comment. "He thinks I'm a threat? To who or what?" There was both confusion and anger on Lauren's face. "I wouldn't do anything to harm Caleb or his family. You all have been so good to me! What type of person does he think I am? He doesn't even know me!" The truth suddenly hit her. "Of course! He doesn't know me! Oh Annie," Lauren softened her voice, "he's just concerned for Caleb and any motives

I might have." She let out a deep sigh. "Do you think I'm after something from Caleb?"

Annie smile at the young woman and knew in her heart that she would never do anything to harm anyone.

"I believe you lass and in time Mr. Whitworth will too. Clean yourself up and come eat with us downstairs. You've been cooped up in this room too long." Annie gave her a reassuring hug and left her to regain her composure.

Lauren knew what she had to do and as soon as Mr. Whitworth returned she would ask to speak with him. If he wanted her to leave she would.

She was glad to have her appetite back when she saw the spread for dinner. Annie certainly knew how to cook. They were about to be seated when Jake entered the house.

He was dusty from the trail and looked tired. As soon as the aroma of the meal hit his nose he smiled. "Annie, my love, you are the best cook in town! I'm glad I decided to come home."

"You won't be sitting at this table until you get washed, we'll wait," she scolded with a smile.

Lauren wondered if Mr. Whitworth was the one who ran Eden or this spunky woman with the wooden spoon in her hand continuously threatening one of his sons. She never heard anyone argue with Annie.

It didn't take long before Jake returned for dinner. He noticed Lauren for the first time. "Lauren, I presume?" he asked her.

She knew this must be Jake. He didn't look much younger than Caleb and was definitely not Evan's twin.

"You presume correctly." Lauren extended her hand toward him. To her surprise he placed a soft kiss on the back of it.

"Oh brother," Caleb said while rolling his eyes. He pulled Lauren's chair out for her. "I can't believe you two. You act like you've never seen a woman before."

"We have, but to have one share our dinner table is rare – with the exception of our lovely Annie, of course," Jake quickly added.

Annie chuckled at his remark and sat down in the chair Evan held for her. "My goodness, what chivalry!" She was tickled and her face was flushed from laughter. She smacked the back of Evan's hand when he started for a juicy piece of roast. "You know we give thanks to the Almighty before we eat." Evan blushed as he bowed his head.

"Thank you, Lord for blessing us and caring for us. We ask that you look after the ones who are not with us tonight. Bless this food to our bodies and thank you for bringing Miss Lauren to our home. Amen." Annie lifted her head and addressed Evan. "Now, if you would please pass the serving platters around the table young man and not attack the food like it's going to run from ya!"

Everyone laughed at her teasing. Evan's face turned red again as he joined in the laughter.

Lauren was touched that Annie remembered her in the prayer and wondered if this was merely a tradition or if she truly meant the words. She made a mental note to ask her later but in the meantime she allowed herself to enjoy dinner with all of them.

They relived their childhood pranks they played on each other and had Annie and Lauren in tears from laughing so hard.

Caleb thought Lauren never looked prettier as she smiled and joked with them.

"The Independence Day picnic is coming next Saturday, are you going to ask Sally Ann?" Evan's asked Jake.

"That is none of your business," he scolded his brother.

"What about you Caleb? Are you going to take Lauren?"

Caleb was completely caught off guard and choked on his water. "I don't think I'll be around, it's my turn to watch the herds." He didn't want to give the family the wrong impression when it came to the two of them. She was a guest and that was all.

"Then I'll take her!" Evan gladly offered.

Lauren blushed and didn't know what to say. Annie came to her rescue. "She'll be going with me so you can escort the two of us." This wasn't exactly what Evan had in mind but it would have to do. Lauren gave a thankful glance toward Annie. "Do you feel up to helping me with the dishes?" Annie asked Lauren.

"Yes." She welcomed the chance to escape after Evan's proposal.

The two of them cleared the table and cleaned the dinner dishes. When they were done they sat in the kitchen and enjoyed a cup of tea together. Annie was fond of Lauren and she was going to miss her when she returned to her home. Deep down; she knew that Lauren was running from something or someone. When she was delirious with fever she often fought with someone in her dreams. This gave her the impression she was afraid of being hurt. She was going to have to think of some way to keep this young lady in Eden. She needed them. Why? She wasn't sure but the Lord put had put Lauren in this family for a reason.

Chapter Ten

The last week of June brought hot weather. The windows were opened in the house to let the fresh air flow through all the rooms but it didn't always bring the relief needed from the stuffiness.

Lauren missed the cool breezes that blew in from sea and the smell of the salt water. She did whatever chore she could outside during the day where it was cooler. Her mind wandered from one thought to the next as she took the dry laundry from the line. She wondered what condition she'd find her father's business in when she returned. She was afraid to let anyone know where she was in case her uncle questioned them.

She came across one of Caleb's shirts and held it close to inhale the fresh scent. She closed her eyes and imagined the strong arms that held her when she was sick. She didn't hear the footsteps behind her and was startled when a deep voice interrupted her daydreaming.

"Do you inspect all the clothes that closely?"

She turned so fast to see who was speaking that she tripped over the laundry basket. Two strong arms kept her from tumbling. Standing in front of her was a tall, handsome man that was no doubt Caleb's father. Lauren could feel her face burn with embarrassment and quickly dropped the shirt in the basket.

"No sir." She was so flustered she didn't know whether to continue with the laundry or face this man who studied her. "I was just thinking about my home." She regained some of her composure and stood up straight with her chin in the air. *It's now or never.* She offered her hand to the man whose eyes bore through her. "Mr. Whitworth, I am Lauren Bailey. It is a pleasure to finally meet you." She felt like a fool with her hand outstretched until he finally took it in his. "I want to thank you for allowing me to stay here."

"That was more my son's idea than mine." He showed no emotion.

"Yes, I know and I'm so sorry to barge in like this." Remembering his accusations gave her the boldness she needed to defend herself. "I know that you think I'm using your son and taking advantage of your hospitality. All you have to do is tell me to leave and I will, but I want you to know that I *never* had any intentions to harm Caleb or anyone else in your family."

Will didn't know she was aware of his suspicions and was at a loss for words.

Lauren took advantage of his silence and continued. "If you allow me to stay. I promise I'll not be a burden to any of you and I'll help with any chore given to me to repay your kindness."

Will was taken back by this little spit fire of a woman. He gave her credit for standing up to him. He was beginning to understand why his son was so taken with her; she was very beautiful, with her dark hair, small stature and light blue eyes. She reminded him of one of the porcelain dolls they sold at the mercantile.

"I hope that what you say is true. As far as asking you to leave I'm afraid that Annie will hang me if I do. She's told me how much you do to help. I appreciate it. Now if you'll excuse me."

When he was out of sight Lauren flopped down on the basket of clothes relieved.

"Thank you Lord! Thank you so much! Please continue to show me how to be a servant to this wonderful family!"

Will followed the sound of a hammer pounding against metal. He knew he'd find Caleb working with the horses. He smiled at the thought of Lauren holding Caleb's shirt and wondered if his son had any idea about her feelings for him. She was something else and he couldn't help but like her even though it was their first encounter. He warned himself not to let his guard down until he received the response to a telegraph he sent to the Cape Jennings' sheriff's office.

Caleb was clothed in leather chaps and bib pounding an iron shoe into shape when Will found him. Caleb stopped in mid swing when he saw his pa approach. He took a handkerchief and wiped the sweat off his hands and face.

"Pa," he acknowledged then picked up the hammer to continue his work.

"I met your young lady." Will announced.

"She's not my young lady, she's a guest here." Caleb answered between swings not looking at his pa.

"I told her she was welcomed to stay as long as she needed." Will walked away not waiting for a response.

Caleb couldn't believe what he had just heard. He sought out Lauren to find out what had happened between the two. "What did you say to my pa?" he asked when he found her.

Lauren looked at him and her heart stopped. His shirt was unbuttoned and the sleeves where rolled up above the elbows allowing full view of the muscles in his forearms. The bibs didn't cover his entire chest and the dark chest hair glistened from sweat. The sight of him took her breath away.

"Lauren?" he asked again. "What did you say to my pa?"

She snapped her mouth shut and hoped he didn't notice her staring at him. She quickly turned and busied herself with the laundry hoping to hide her flaming face. "Nothing, I just thanked him for letting me stay here and told him that if I caused any problems I'd leave."

"That's it?"

"Yes," she looked over her shoulder, "and that I'll help anyway I can around here."

"Hun..." was the only comment he made before he went back to work.

"I'll be darned..." Caleb thought to himself, *"first my brothers and now pa."* He smiled and went back to work whistling.

Lauren finally managed to get the laundry in the house after all the interruptions and helped

Annie with dinner. She was introduced to Ethan and noticed he was a bit shorter than Evan and had lighter hair. He wasn't as rambunctious as Evan when he was alone but, when his brother was around there was constant competition keeping everyone entertained.

The strain between Will and Caleb lessened and they talked with Jake on the porch where it was cool until they were called in for dinner. Annie gave the blessing as she did every night before anyone was allowed to eat. The conversation was pleasant and once again everyone was laughing at tales from the past.

Annie cleared her throat to get Will's attention. "I was wondering if I can use the wagon tomorrow to go to town."

"I'll be headed that way if you want me to pick something up for you," Jake offered.

"Thank you, but I thought I'd take Lauren with me to pick out some fabric, the poor dear's been wearing the same dress since she's been here." Annie didn't lift her eyes confident that she'd get her way. "Besides, she'll need something for the picnic Saturday."

Lauren felt every eye on her. She wanted to crawl under the table.

"That'll be fine. Jake you go with them and keep them out of trouble." This was the first time Lauren saw Will smile.

"Thank you but there's no need to...." Lauren tried to talk Annie out of her generosity but she wouldn't hear of it.

"Nonsense, if you wear that dress any longer it'll walk to the wash tub on its own," Annie said.

Lauren laughed along with the rest of them.

After dinner everyone went their own way to relax for the rest of the evening. Lauren and Annie talked about styles and patterns and maybe even lunch at Sally Ann's. After a list of items they'd need was completed, Lauren excused herself early and went to her room to write a letter to her father's lawyer in Cape Jennings.

June 29, 1884

Dear Mr. Hobbs,

I am staying near a town called Clayton's Creek in Oregon. I assure you I am being well cared for by a wonderful family. I ask that you keep my location quiet from my uncle. As you know his greed will no doubt have him headed this way if he finds out I'm here. I have a dreadful feeling he wants to claim my inheritance; which brings me to another matter. I recently married a very good man but only to keep from having to return to my uncle if he finds me. His family is not aware of this arrangement. I don't want any harm to come to my husband or his family.

I need to get all my father's affairs in order. If you could please write to me and help me with the estate and shipping business, I will forever be in your debt.

Please give Mrs. Hobbs a hug for me and tell her I am safe. I miss you very much and I hope I haven't caused you too much worry.

You can send all correspondences to me at Clayton's Creek, Oregon and I'm sure I'll get it.

Praying for you always,

Lauren Bailey

She prayed over the letter and asked God to get it to Cape Jennings quickly. As much as she hated to, she'd have to ask Annie for money for the postage. She'd work extra hard for it in return. She thought about the outing the next day and could hardly wait to pick out fabric. How sweet they've all been to her, even Mr. Whitworth seemed to be warming a little toward her. For the first time in months, Lauren slept peacefully.

Lauren woke the next morning to a soft breeze blowing in her window and across her bed. She stretched lazily and listened to the birds outside her window. She remembered she was going to town with Annie and jumped out of bed. She was so excited she felt like a child on Christmas morning. It was amazing how much better she felt after Annie's care and wonderful food. She hung the dress Caleb bought her by the window the night before to let it air. She dusted it with scented powder she found in a small decorative box in one of the guest rooms. She held it to her nose, hoping it wasn't offensive. She was relieved when all she could smell was the powder. She had washed, dressed, and was brushing her hair when someone knocked on her door.

"Come in."

Caleb came in dressed for the trail. "I wanted to give you some money for today." He handed her some folded bills and turned to leave.

"You don't have to do that," Lauren said as she stared at the money.

"I want to." Was all he said and was down the hall before she could return it to him.

Lauren didn't know what to do with the money and wondered if being married to her he felt responsible for her needs. She would talk to him when he came back and let him know that he didn't need to worry about her and remind him the marriage was paper only.

She showed the money to Annie after breakfast when they were alone. "What should I do? I can't take this."

"That was nice of him! You've been work'n hard lass, you deserve it, so be thankful."

Annie was right. She worked from the time she got up until the dinner was cleared. She didn't mind though, it's the least she could do in return for their hospitality. She gave the money to Annie to hold and they headed to the yard. Jake was outside waiting for them in the wagon.

"We'll be eating at Sally Ann's if you want to join us," Annie mentioned to him.

"Ah Annie, still the match maker. We are friends and that's all, so you can play cupid on another couple." He glanced Lauren's way but she was busy making sure her dress wasn't near the wagon wheel. The comment went unheard. Annie just smiled and winked at him.

This was the first time Lauren left Eden. She couldn't believe the beauty of its surrounding. Jake and Annie pointed out different land marks and places of interest. She was in awe when she saw a large lake with the reflection of the mountains on the glassy surface. It was so perfect it looked like a painting.

"What a beautiful place!" she exclaimed.

"That's Lake Eden," Jake told her. "My ma named it. We used to picnic here when she was alive."

"You don't come here anymore?" Lauren asked.

"We fish here once in awhile but pa doesn't come out here. It brings back sad memories. He gave the piece on this side to Caleb and I have the land on the other side." He nodded his head in the direction of his land.

"Can we stop for a minute? It's absolutely breathtaking."

"I don't see why not." Jake stopped the wagon and helped the ladies.

Lauren sat in a patch of clover and breathed in the sweetness of the little purple flowers. Annie and Jake watched her as she closed her eyes and lifted her face to the sun.

"I can feel the Lord's presence here," Lauren said softly.

Annie sat next to her and touched her arm. "Are you a believer, Lauren?"

"Yes, I am. I was nine when I accepted Christ as my savior." She was smiling at Annie. Her question about her spiritual beliefs had been answered. Not many unsaved people used the term *believer.*

"Praise God!" Annie hugged Lauren. "This is wonderful!"

They started chatting back and forth about when they were saved and church when Jake cleared his throat to remind them they were headed somewhere.

"Oh!" Annie giggled. "I'm sorry lad, we're coming."

They got back in the wagon and Jake shook his head as he listened to the non-stop talk about God and being *saved.* He wasn't sure what it was all about and wasn't certain if he even wanted to know.

The threesome arrived to see that the town's folk were preparing for the Independence Day picnic and dance with red, white, and blue banners and flags.

Lauren could feel the excitement and her face lit up as she took in every detail around her. She didn't notice when Jake pulled the wagon to a stop in front of the mercantile.

"Here ya go ladies," he said as he offered his hand in assistance. "I'll see you at Sally Ann's around noon. Don't be late," he threatened with a smile.

"I'm sure you won't be lonely if we are," Annie sassed back.

The mercantile was bigger than it appeared from the outside. Lauren didn't know where to start looking.

"May I help you?" Lauren was approached by a red headed young lady that looked to be in her late teens.

"Good morning Samantha!" Annie greeted her with a hug and a smile. "This is Lauren Bailey and we're here to purchase fabric for some new dresses. What can you show us?"

"Good morning Miss Annie! It's so good to see you." The excitement sparkled in Samantha's green eyes as she addressed Annie. "We just received a new shipment of cotton the other day; come let me show you. Oh!, I'm sorry. Please forgive me. It's a pleasure to meet you Lauren." Her sweet freckled face blushed from her unintentional rudeness.

"It's nice to meet you too," Lauren answered as she laughed. "There are so many beautiful items in here." Lauren was amazed at the selection around her.

"Wait until you see what's back here!" Samantha almost squealed.

She led the women to a back room filled with bolts of various fabrics, lace on one wall, and rolls of ribbons and thread along another. Windows lined the exterior wall letting bright light in the room giving it a cheerful atmosphere.

They pulled down bolts and held them up for Lauren to examine. They went from fabric to lace then back again laughing and exchanging ideas.

"Oh no," Samantha whispered.

Lauren looked up to see a beautiful blonde woman enter the room. She held her head high and walked with authority as she approached the group.

"Miss Annie, how good it is to see you! What brings you to town?" she questioned Annie but was looking at the dark haired woman with her.

"Cynthia Redding, this is Lauren Bailey. She'll be staying with us for awhile." Annie watched over Lauren like a mother hen. Annie never liked Cynthia or her sneaky ways. She'd been after Caleb from the time they went to school together. She knew she would go to any length to get him.

"Aren't you the lucky one to be out there with all those handsome men?" She walked around Lauren eyeing her from head to toe. "I do hope you're a sharing girl."

Lauren's face lit up in anger and was about to voice her opinion when Cynthia quickly turned her attention to Samantha.

"Samantha dear, did that fabric come in that I ordered?" Her overly sweet manner turned Lauren's stomach.

"Yes ma'am, I'll bring it to the counter." Samantha was glad to have an excuse to leave the trio. Cynthia always had a way of making her feel small.

"Will I be seeing you at the picnic?" Cynthia asked Annie and Lauren.

"We'll be there," was all Annie offered. She knew what Cynthia really wanted to know was if Caleb was going to be there.

"Very good, I guess I'll see you Saturday. It was very nice meeting you – Lori."

"Lauren," Annie and Lauren corrected together.

"Yes, Lauren." Cynthia exited as haughty as she entered.

"That woman. Oooo, she makes my blood boil." Annie didn't hold back her true feelings.

"Who is she?" Lauren asked.

"A woman looking for an easy hand out. You stay away from her, she'll bring you noth'n but trouble that one will."

Lauren hugged Annie. "I'm not a little girl but I thank you for the warning. Why don't we get Samantha to wrap our things while we head over to Sally Ann's? I believe I've gotten my appetite back, I'm starving!" She was trying to bring Annie back to her jolly self.

"After you." Annie motioned for her to lead the way.

"I'm afraid it will have to be - after you; I don't know where we're going!" Lauren reminded her.

They both left laughing and in a better mood.

Lauren and Annie found Jake sitting at a table talking with another pretty blonde. The woman saw them enter and practically ran to Annie to hug her.

"Annie! You're here! I've missed you so much." She glanced at the young woman with her. "You must be Lauren. Jake's told me all about you. I'm Sally Ann, welcome to Clayton's Creek."

She surprised Lauren with a hug. It was a much nicer greeting than the one she received from Cynthia.

"I hope Jake was kind in what he told you," Lauren teased.

"Yes, he was and I wouldn't believe him if he wasn't." She looked at Jake as she spoke.

Lauren noticed the tender way he looked at her and smiled. She was a lucky woman to have his affection. Jake was a good man, all the Whitworth's were good men. She understood why Cynthia tried so hard to win one of their hearts.

"Do you run this place by yourself?" Lauren asked.

The dining room was very elegant but not overly decorated. She didn't want to drive the male customers away.

"I not only run it, I own it. My parents left it to me when they moved back east. I didn't want to go back with them so I took over the business and I'm glad. I love it here." Jake was watching her making her blush. "Well, if you'll excuse me. I'll bring you some refreshments." She needed to leave the room. Her emotions from Jake eyeing her caused her to become flustered.

"Jake! You're awful!" Annie scolded but there was a little mischief behind her eyes as well. "You had her running like a scared rabbit!"

"I can't help it, she's the most beautiful thing I've ever seen; I can't take my eyes off her." Jake let out a hearty laugh.

"Then you need to marry her and get it over with instead of stringing her along ike you do. You can at least ask her to the picnic on Saturday."

"You'll be glad to know I did that very thing before you got here. She'll be open for lunch then I'll have her the rest of the day."

"What about you, Lauren? Will you save me a dance? That is, of course, if you can squeeze me in."

"What do you mean by that?" Lauren asked confused.

"Don't you know? You're the talk of the town. Everyone wants to see the mysterious woman Caleb brought home with him. You should hear the stories." He shook his head and tried to hide his smile behind his drink.

"No! You're not serious! Are you?" She wasn't sure she liked the idea of being the topic of town.

"Jacob Whitworth – if you don't stop with the teasing I'll tell Sally Ann every embarrassing moment of your life; starting with that incident at the creek and a fish hook..." Annie said.

"You are ruthless, Annie. I give." Jake had a look of defeat on his face. "But Lauren is the talk of town."

Annie saw the concerned look on Lauren's face. "Ah, it's a small town, lass. It doesn't take much to get them talk'n. Don't fret about it." She squeezed Lauren's hand.

Lauren took her advice and was determined not to let the gossiping ruin her day.

Sally Ann had their lunch brought to the table and joined them when she could between customers. Annie informed her that Lauren was a believer and Sally Ann made Annie promise to bring her to the bible studies they held on Wednesday afternoons.

When they were done eating, they said their goodbyes and headed to the mercantile. On the way Lauren remembered her letter to Mr. Hobbs.

"Where can I post a letter?" she asked. She noticed the confused look on Annie's face. "It's to my father's lawyer. I need to tend to some of his business."

"I'm sorry, you must think I'm a busy body, it's just around the corner. You post your letter and I'll get our goods from Samantha. Jake'll be here in a minute with the wagon. I can't wait to get home to start sewing!"

Lauren laughed at her new friend's excitement but had to admit she couldn't wait to get back to the ranch either.

She walked to the post office as fast as she could. She noticed the stares directed toward her but thought she was being self conscious after Jake's comment. She brushed it off and went on with her business.

She met Jake and Annie in front of the mercantile and they headed home. *Home* she thought to herself. How easy it was for her to refer to Eden as home. She felt sad when she remembered she'd be there for only a few more months. She knew she'd miss all of them when she left. The thought of not seeing Caleb anymore sent a sinking feeling in her chest. She tried to brush it away and think about the sewing and new dresses instead.

The ride home was pleasant until they arrived home. Lauren and Annie heard Will's bellowing voice as they entered the yard.

"The subject is closed! I won't hear of it again!"

113

Ethan stomped out of the house and slammed the door behind him before heading down the path toward the creek.

"Oh, dear," Annie whispered under her breath. "When will that man learn he's gonna hold him so tight he'll lose him forever?"

"I've tried talking to Pa. It's no use," Jake told her.

"He's too stubborn for his own good. Do you need help with the packages?" Jake asked Lauren.

"I have them, thanks. Is everything okay Annie?"

"No, it's the same thing every time Ethan brings up the subject about going to school. His pa won't have anything to do with it – *tis a waste of time!* – He says. He's smothering the poor lad."

"Why is he so against it?" Lauren couldn't imagine anyone not wanting their child to further their education to better themselves.

"Ethan needs to study for an entrance exam or something like that and Will won't hire a tutor to help him. He says it's a waste of money and time and that he's needed on the range. Poppy cock!"

"He's home every night, I can help him study," Lauren offered.

"Tis no use lass, he won't have it." Annie stomped in the house mumbling under her breath.

Lauren stood in the doorway deep in thought. She put her bundle of goods on a chair and followed the path she saw Ethan take. She found him leaning against a tree pulling leaves off a branch.

"Ethan?" She approached carefully not knowing what to expect.

"What do you want?" he barked at her. "Did pa send you down here to get me?"

"No, I'm sorry I heard the arguing and Annie told me what it was about." He jerked his head up to look at her. "I know it's none of my business but I think I have an idea that might help," she dared to continue.

"It's no use, he won't let me go. I just don't get it! He won't even listen to me, it's not like I'll be gone forever. When I watch pa help a mare give birth it amazes me at how skilled he is and the beauty of the whole thing. It makes me want to know more. I want to be able to help the ones he can't because he doesn't know what to do. There's a whole world out there other then branding and roping but I can't get him to see past that. I want to learn about medicine, I want to be a veterinarian and use it here at Eden and the neighboring ranches." He let out a deep sigh before continuing. "But, I don't know if I'm smart enough to pass the exam to get into the school. He won't hire anyone to help me."

"I can help you," Lauren told him. "If you can get your pa to let you take the test I'll help you study for it. If you pass, maybe he'll let you further your education. If you don't pass, at least you tried and you can tell him you're done with it."

"But I don't want to be done with it, I want to pass." He was broken and it hurt Lauren to see his pain.

"Then we need to make sure you pass the exam!" Lauren gave him a friendly nudge.

He looked at her with hope in his eyes and wondered how his brother could be so blind to her beauty; not only her external beauty, but the beauty that shone from within.

"I'll pray about it and you talk to your pa but don't get angry – that won't help," she advised.

"If you think praying will help go for it and pray hard!" He was feeling a little better.
"If he agrees to the terms, we can study for an hour or two every night after dinner but you have to be serious about this," she warned.

"I've never been more serious about anything." The yearning in his eyes was enough to convince Lauren.

They walked back to the house together making plans hoping Will would agree with them. Lauren shared their idea with Annie and they agreed to both pray hard about it for Ethan's sake.

Ethan decided he'd wait awhile before bringing up the school subject again to give his pa's temper time to simmer down. He asked Samantha to order the study book for him. He put in an extra effort while working so he could stay on Will's good side. He knew his pa loved him but he'd be eighteen in a couple months and it was time to go after his dream of becoming a veterinarian. He also knew he didn't want to be a rancher the rest of his life. His brothers would work the ranch long after their pa was gone. He'd still be close at hand whenever he was needed but his dreams took him down another path.

Chapter Eleven

The week flew by quickly. Lauren and Annie were successful in completing two dresses. They had spent the entire day Friday on housework and preparing the baskets for the picnic. Saturday everyone was up early and ready to head for town by mid morning.

Lauren descended the stairs in a light green and pink dress. The short sleeves were puffed and trimmed with lace to match the pink rosebud buttons. She pulled her hair back and tied it with a small ribbon. Her face was flushed and her eyes were bright with excitement.

Everyone was helping Annie load the buggy when Lauren made her appearance on the stairs. The men stopped in their tracks when they saw the vision before them.

"Wow Lauren! You sure do clean up nice!" Evan teased her.

Her laughter added to her beauty. "Not bad yourself!" She gave him a friendly shove. "If you're nice I might let you dance with me."

"Not if you value your toes! But on the other hand if you dance with me, you'll feel like you're dancing on clouds," Ethan assured her.

"I think I'm gonna have to do some target practice and use the two of you for the targets," Jake said while he watched his brothers make fools out of themselves. He couldn't blame them though. He wished Caleb was there to see her shine. He grew to think of Lauren like a sister and cared for her very much. He knew he'd defend her honor if he had to since his brother was never around. The gossip around town wasn't always in her favor. He hoped the meddling women would keep civil tongues and allow her to have a good day. He was sure Annie and Sally Ann would be with her most of the time.

The thought of Sally Ann made him hustle his family along. He wanted to see her as much as possible. "Let's move'm out!" he yelled. "Get that basket from Annie and let's go. Pa's waiting for us."

"I'm sorry Annie; I should have been down here helping you." Lauren took the blankets Annie had draped over her arm.

"That's alright lass; there are plenty of idol folks around here that can help." She slapped Evan on his behind to hurry him along. "My Lauren, don't you look pretty. You'll not lack for a dance partner tonight – that's for sure."

Lauren smiled and hugged her. "Thanks to you!"

"Come now," Annie said blushing.
That was the first time Lauren saw Annie blush and it tickled her to see she wasn't as tough as she tried to make everyone think she was.

Will was mounted, ready to go leading a beautiful two year old he planned to race that day. "You didn't forget the apple pie did you because I'll make all of you turn around to get it," Will warned. He was dressed in a freshly pressed white shirt with a black tie. He was clean shaven and even his boots were polished.

Lauren thought of Caleb when she looked at him and wondered if he'd be as handsome when he was his pa's age. Deep down she wished he was there with them. She had the feeling he had been avoiding her.

****

Caleb was rounding up stray cattle when Kent rode up beside him. The sun was already beating down without mercy. Sweat ran down their faces makeing streaks from the caked on dust.

"You need to be with your family. Take the day off Caleb, its quiet and there's plenty of help out here, go on, get out'ta here." Kent had noticed that Caleb was spending more time on the range than he normally did. He wondered if the woman he had brought home had anything to do with it. She was pretty and from what he heard she was just as sweet.

"I'm fine. They know I'm not going and won't miss me." Caleb thought about Lauren and wondered if she would miss him.

"Come on! You'd rather be out here than danc'n with that purdy gal of yours? The sun's done some damage to your thinking." Kent said as he shook his head. "I'll be there later; me and the boys are taking shifts so we can all go. Ride back with me."

"Number one; she's not *my* gal, number two; I'm sure she'll have plenty of partners and three…"

"There is no three, admit it," Kent said. He wasn't going to give up on his friend. "I've seen the way you look at her so don't tell me *she's not your gal.* If you don't wanna go fine, I'll just dance with her all night. Who knows — she might like my company better!" He rode off before Caleb could retaliate. "*That ought to light a fire under him,*" Kent thought to himself.

"You all need to mind your own business!" Caleb shouted at Kent's back. "I'll go if I want to, not because I'm being roped into it!"

****

As the Eden group approached town they heard laughter, music, and someone speaking through a megaphone. They found a shady spot under an oak to tie the horses for the day. Between all of them they were able to gather all the baskets and blankets and sought out a place to set up for lunch.

Lauren was so excited she could barley sit long enough to eat. When they were done eating, Annie walked with her through town to introduce her to families from the church. Some of the women looked down their noses at her. She just smiled.

Annie saw the hurt in her eyes from the cold stares. "Don't let it bother you lass. They're the ones who have nothing better to do than mind other people's business. I got the same treatment when I moved in after me Robert passed. They pegged me as a gold digger - after wealth and glamour."

Lauren was shocked that anyone could think such a thing about Annie. She was such a sweet woman. "What did you do?" Lauren asked.

"I prayed about it and let the Lord take care of it for me and eventually the gossip stopped. They eventually saw that I only needed a place to live and that Will needed help. I believe our God worked that all out for us." Annie gave her a reassuring hug and put her arm in hers. "Let's look at the quilts, shall we?"

They walked up and down the wooden boardwalk looking at quilts, dresses, crocheted doilies and many other beautiful hand worked items.

"Lauren! Annie!" Sally Ann was walking with Jake when she spotted the two women. She hugged both of them.

"I thought you were going to open the café today," Lauren said.

"I changed my mind. It's such a beautiful day I couldn't stand it any longer so I closed right after breakfast." She glanced at Jake. "It didn't help that I was taken hostage either!"

"I don't recall you putting up much of a fight." He smiled at her then remembered they weren't alone. "I must leave you lovely ladies and find pa. He's racing Blaze of Thunder so I better find out if he needs me to ride." He placed a soft kiss on the back of Sally Ann's hand then winked at Lauren and Annie. "Ladies." He tipped his hat then went on his way.

Sally Ann turned five shades of red causing Annie and Lauren to laugh at her flustered state.

"Oh! To be in love again," Annie chuckled.

"Who said anything about love?" Sally Ann asked fanning herself.

"Las, if you can't see it then you need glasses!"

Jake found Will in the livery brushing Blaze. He was humming a song he remembered his ma singing to him when he was younger.

Will had a soothing touch when it came to the horses. He wondered why it was so hard for him to show the same affection toward his family.

"Hey Pa." Jake grabbed the halter and stroked Blaze's soft muzzle. "She's looking good. Do you want me to ride?"

"I've been checking things out and I bet we'll have a better chance if we let Ev. He's smaller then the rest of the riders I've seen, what do you think?" Will asked.

"Can he handle her?" Evan was good but he had never raced. Jake knew his pa had some money bet on Blaze.

"I think he'll do fine." He stepped back and admired the gleaming coat on the horse. Neither one heard Tim enter the livery.

"She's beautiful, Will. If I was a bet'n man I'd have my money on her. You riding her Jake?" Tim asked.

"Nope, we're gonna put Ev to the test," Jake answered.

"Here," Tim handed Will an envelope, "this came late yesterday afternoon. I would've brought it to ya sooner, but I knew you'd be here today. Hope ya don't mind."

Will glanced at Jake and stuffed the envelope in his back pocket. "That's fine, thanks Tim."

He busied himself with Blaze to try and keep Jake's attention off the letter.

"I'll see ya at the finish line, but right now I believe it's my duty to judge the pies and cakes. A man's got to do what a man's got to do. This is a tough job."

"Then if I were you I'd get at it!" Will said laughing. "Jake, I need you to find Ev so I can go over a few things with him before the race. You'll probably find him by the group of young ladies gathered near the lemonade stand; that's where I saw him last."

"Okay, hope I can tear him away." Jake wondered about the letter but knew that if he was meant to know what was in it, his pa would tell him.

Will waited until he knew Jake had left before he read the letter.

June 19, 1884

Dear Mr. Whitworth,

My name is Lawrence Hobbs and I am the acting attorney for Miss Bailey's family. The sheriff of Cape Jennings received your wire concerning Lauren and he forwarded it to me.

I will assure you that Lauren Bailey is from a fine Christian family. You need not worry about her harming your family. Her family and I have been friends for a long time. I highly respected both her parents.

I don't know if you are aware of the fact that Lauren's parents are no longer alive and she was left at the mercy of her uncle, Henry Bailey. There are suspicions that he had a hand in the deaths of Mr. and Mrs. Bailey but as of today we have no evidence. He and Lauren disappeared shortly after Mrs. Bailey's funeral and until we received your wire we assumed her to be lost. I thank the Lord in knowing that she is safe and away from her uncle.

I wish to extend my deepest gratitude to you and your son for opening your home to her. I have the unfortunate job of telling her that her uncle has left her penniless. He was so far in debt that I had no choice but to sell the business, the ships, and her home. I used her inheritance to pay the filthy hounds he owed. I also had to use money from my own estate to satisfy the loans. She has nothing, no home, money, or family.

I hate to ask you, but if she can stay at least until her 21st birthday my wife and I would greatly appreciate it. Her uncle has one of his rats here looking for her to return and she will not be safe in Cape Jennings. Bailey is not aware of her financial state and I believe he is still thinking he will profit from her inheritance. If you find that you can no longer allow her to stay with your family please write to me and I make arrangements for her as soon as possible. But, as I said earlier, the farther we can keep her away from Cape Jennings the better.

Once again, thank you Mr. Whitworth, for caring for her. If you need anything, please do not hesitate to contact me.

Sincerely,

Lawrence Hobbs

Will folded the letter and put it back in his pocket. After spending time with Lauren over the past few weeks he knew deep down in his heart that she wasn't a threat. He felt guilty for thinking she was. How was he going to tell her about her future? She was hoping to return home but now she had neither home nor money. He decided he wouldn't say anything to her yet. Maybe things would work out where she wouldn't have to leave. How, he wasn't sure, but for now Eden would be her home for as long as she needed it to be. Satisfied with his decision he led Blaze outside and waited for Evan to go over last minute instructions.

Chapter Twelve

Annie, Lauren, and Sally Ann found a place to sit to watch the race. Lauren took in all the sights and sounds; the men waving money in the air to place their bets, the horse and riders getting their final instructions, ladies fanning themselves from the heat of the day and an occasional comment about a horse and its chance of winning. They spotted the Whitworth horse and remarked how beautiful she was.

"She is beautiful but I think my Fly By Night will be the winner." Pierce Compton, the town banker, wandered over to the ladies. He was overly dressed for the occasion in a three piece suite. "Pierce Compton at your service." He bowed in a gentlemanly manner as he introduced himself to Lauren. He completely ignored Annie and Sally Ann. "You must be the mysterious Lauren Bailey I've heard so much about."

Lauren became irritated by his rudeness toward her friends. "I am Lauren Bailey but I don't see why you think I'm a mystery," she asked mockingly.

He took her testy answer as a challenge. He liked women with spunk. "For starters, the stories I've heard about the beauty that moved in with the Whitworth's. Now that I've met you I can see why they want to keep you a secret.

The competition for your attention could get nasty." He smiled at her.

"That will be enough Mr. Compton. Now if you don't mind..." Annie motioned for him to move on. She never liked the pompous man and he knew it.

"Yes, I should attend to my rider. Miss Bailey, if you'd like to wager on my filly I'll place the bet for you?"

"No thank you, sir, I don't believe in gambling," she answered coldly.

"Very well, I hope you will save me a dance tonight." He nodded his head and left.

"The nerve of him!" Sally Ann blurted. "He acted like we weren't even here!"

"I'd welcome the plague before I'd dance with him! Who is he?" Lauren asked.

"He operates the bank but he thinks he owns it," Sally Ann answered. It was obvious she didn't like him either. "I'm glad you're here Lauren, now he'll leave me alone!"

"And me too," Annie agreed.

Sally Ann and Lauren looked at the smiling Annie then started to laugh with her.

"Race starts in five minutes!" Sheriff Poynter announced through the megaphone.

The riders had a one mile track that was marked with spikes and yellow ribbons with the finish line just inside of town. There were five riders lined up ready to go. The horses sensed the anticipation of the riders and pawed at the ground. They were ready to run. Each rider did their best to keep them under control.

"Riders!" Tim yelled into the megaphone.

"Take your marks!" Satisfied they were in line, Tim fired one shot in the air and the horses took off as if Satan himself was on their tails.

The town shouted for their favorite as they tried to pass each other. Blaze of Thunder was second behind Fly by Night. The women shouted their support for Evan. They were a quarter mile from the finish line when Evan let Blaze have her head and she ran with ease past Fly by Night finishing in first place.

Evan was very pleased with himself and Blaze. He gave her an approving pat on her neck and held up his hand in victory.

Will was extremely proud of both and didn't hide it from the crowd. He pulled Evan off the horse and hugged him in front of the entire town.

Jake messed his hair and slapped his back. "Great job Ev!" he shouted above the crowd. "Of course I would've won by two lengths but you still did a good job."

Ethan approached with Samantha by his side. "Congratulations!" they said almost in unison. Ev just smiled loving all the attention.

After the excitement died down, Will brought Blaze back to the livery. He then met his family at the picnic area for dinner. They relaxed until it started to get dark and listened while the musicians warmed up for the dance.

Will watched Lauren as she blended in with his family so easily. She had managed to find a soft spot in his heart and he hated to have to tell her what he found out from Hobbs. His boys accepted her as one of the family. He knew that Jake would eventually ask Sally Ann to marry him and from what he observed, Ethan was falling for Samantha. It was Caleb that had him confused. Why did he avoid her like he did? He witnessed the tender way he cared for her when she was sick and how he followed her with his eyes when he thought no one was looking. If he didn't know better, he'd say Caleb was in love with her.

Will's thoughts were interrupted when his family headed toward the dance platform. It didn't take long for them to join in with the dancing. The fiddle player played with a vengeance to keep up with the caller.

"Swing your partner!" He was clapping and stomping his feet keeping time with the music. "Promenade left!"

Lauren didn't know the dance. She had Evan, her partner, laughing while she tried to keep up with the calls.

Ethan and Samantha were in their line so Lauren did her best to follow Samantha. By the time the dance was over they were all flushed from promenading and swinging. Lauren flopped down on the wooden bench next to Annie who was laughing at the catastrophe they called dancing.

"I declare! That was a disaster!" she managed to say while laughing.

"Oh Annie! I never felt like such a fool!" Lauren giggled.

Ethan and Evan brought drinks to the girls. The next song was slower and allowed the dancers to catch their breath.

"Come on Annie, your turn." Ethan grabbed her arm and led her to dance.

"Miss Lauren, may I have the honor of this dance?" Pierce Compton held his hand out for Lauren to take.

"Thank you, Mr. Compton, but I think I'll sit this one out. The last one almost killed me." She hoped that her declining him would make him move on to someone else but he was insistent.

"I'll be easy on you, it's slow."

Before she could decline again he pulled her to her feet and they were among the other dancers. She looked around for her companions but they were already dancing and didn't notice her troubled state.

Pierce didn't take his eyes off her while they danced and it made her very uncomfortable. He tried to impress her by using big words and brag about his position at the bank. Each word out of his mouth was laced with alcohol.

She tried to turn her head to avoid the rancid smell but it was useless. She thought the music would never end. When it did she thanked him and quickly departed from him. She looked up and saw Caleb standing among his brothers watching her. Her heart skipped a beat when he smiled in her direction. She started toward him and stopped as soon as she saw Cynthia by his side.

"Caleb! I didn't think you'd be here tonight!" Cynthia stood on tip toes and shamefully placed a kiss on his mouth.

Lauren turned away from the scene and headed in the opposite direction.

"Where you going in such a hurry lass?" Annie asked.

"I need to freshen up," she stammered.

"Go to the hotel, they have a room set aside for the ladies. Do you need me to show you?"

"No, that's okay, I'll find it."

Without looking back she made her way down the street toward the hotel. She concluded that Cynthia was the reason he'd been staying away. She was heartbroken. She never thought he was involved with someone when they met. He never said anything to her. When they were together he treated her as if he cared for her more than just a friend.

She was deep in thought and didn't notice the shadow lurking between the buildings. An arm reached out and pulled her from the boardwalk pinning her against the building. She hit the wall with such force it knocked the wind out of her.

"Did you think I'd let you go so easily?" Pierce whispered in her ear. "I'm sure those Whitworth brothers won't mind sharing. Which one will it be tonight? Maybe after you spend some time with me you won't want to go back with them."

She couldn't believe what he was implying. Was this what the folks around here thought about her? She tried to yell but her voice was caught in her throat. The harder she struggled to free herself the tighter his grip grew. He smelled her hair then started to place his filthy lips on her neck.

"No!" she finally managed to scream. She gathered what strength she could to get him off of her but it just made him laugh. The only weapon she had were her teeth. She bit him as hard as she could on his shoulder.

"AAAAH! Why you ....."

Before she could get away he hit her across the face with the back of his hand. She took advantage of his loosened grip and tried to run. He grabbed her by her hair. She let out a cry of pain when he pulled her back slamming her against the wall.

"God help me! Please God don't let this be happening!"

As quickly as he grabbed her he let her go. She fell on her knees not comprehending the commotion around her.

The sound of flesh hitting flesh filled her ears. Then there was silence. A hand gently touched her shoulder causing her to jump and cry out in fear.

"No!" She slapped at the hand and tried to rise to her feet but she was stepping on her dress and couldn't stand.

"Lauren! It's Caleb. It's okay, I'm here." He tried to sooth her but she was beyond being calm. She felt dirty and didn't want him touching her.

"Let go of me," she spat.

Caleb was shocked at the venom in her voice and just looked at her. "Are you hurt?" he asked.

"No, I just want to leave – now!" She finally managed to get to her feet and steadied herself. Caleb reached out to help her but she shook his hand from her. "Take me home," she insisted.

"Alright, I need to let them know we're leaving. I'll take you to the wagon first," he told her.

"Don't tell them what happened." This wasn't a plea; it was a demand.

"They're gonna want to know why."

"Don't tell them!" She headed to the street. She stopped when she saw Pierce laying on his back knocked out cold. His face was bruised and bloodied.

Caleb tried to usher her past him but as soon as he put his hand on the small of her back she moved away from him.

"I can find my way," she said flatly. She left him staring at her back.

He didn't know what he had done to make her so angry with him. He hurried to his family and told them he was taking her home. He told them she wasn't feeling well.

Annie offered to go too but he told her that he'd take her and that she needn't worry. He found Lauren hiding in the shadow of the tree where the horses were tied. They'd have to double on his so Annie could use the wagon. He helped Lauren to the saddle then jumped up behind her. She sat rigid trying not to lean on him.

"I'm sorry, Lauren. Please tell me you're okay," he pleaded softly.

She wouldn't answer him. She looked straight ahead and ignored any attempt he made to talk to her.

He went to the dance to be with her. When he saw her smile at him he thought she was happy to see him but then she disappeared. When Annie told him she had gone to the hotel he couldn't believe she let her go alone. He went to find her and was glad he did. When he saw Pierce with his hands all over her, he had to control the urge to kill him. Without thinking he tried to hold Lauren close to him but she

133

stiffened bringing him back to reality.

"This whole thing is my fault. If I was there none of this would have happened."

"But you weren't," she said angrily.

The truth in her words hit him like a ton of bricks. He hadn't been there to keep her safe like he promised her he would. Tonight he realized that she needed protection from more than her uncle.

Neither one spoke the rest of the way to the ranch. When they arrived, Lauren jumped down before he could help her and slammed the front door. He let her go knowing it was no use to try and talk to her.

****

A woman's scream caused the musicians to stop playing. Pierce, bloodied and bruised, tried to make his way back to the crowd.

"What happened?" Tim asked while he assisted the staggering man.

"It was that Bailey woman. She lured me in the alley then had Caleb Whitworth jump me." Pierce let out an exaggerated moan as he tried to sit.

"That's a lie!" Will shouted. "Why would they do such a preposterous thing?" Will's eyes bore holes through Pierce.

"I don't know! Maybe he was jealous because I danced with her!" Pierce shouted back.

"Someone get the doctor! Will, where's Caleb and Lauren?" Tim asked.

"He took Lauren home because she wasn't feeling well." Will quickly realized the mistake in answering him in front of the town. He envisioned what was going through their active imaginations. "Boys, we're going home, help Annie get everything loaded."

"You won't mind if I ride out with you to get their side of the story do you?" Tim asked.

"You honestly don't believe this weasel do you?" Will asked while pointing at Pierce.

"I have to do my job," Tim reminced him.

"Come on then. Let's get to the bottom of this. Boys! You heard me. Let's go!" Will leaned close to Pierce's face. The alcohol was heavy on the man's breath. "If I find out you're behind all this I'll be back to finish what Caleb started!"

****

Caleb tapped on Lauren's bedroom door. "I made you some tea; I'll leave it here for you."

Lauren heard the rattling of the china as he placed the tray on the small table in the hall. He was headed down the stairs when Will and the rest of the family barged through the door. Tim quietly entered behind them.

"What's this all about?" he asked them.

"We were hoping you could tell us," Tim said. "Pierce Compton said that you and Lauren jumped him in the ally in town; I need to hear what happened from you."

"You're joking right?" Caleb couldn't believe what he had just heard.

"'Fraid not, that's what he told the town," Will answered.

Caleb told Lauren he wouldn't tell them what happened but he saw he didn't have a choice.

"I went looking for her and I found Pierce

attacking her in the alley! He was all over her trying to…" he stopped, embarrassed for Lauren's sake, "only God knows what he would have done if I hadn't shown up."

"The poor dear!" Annie headed for the stairs.

"None of this would have happened if you didn't let her go alone to the hotel!" Caleb's anger was directed toward Annie.

"Hold on Caleb!" It was Jake who defended Annie. "None of this would have happened if you didn't dump her and run! You have no right talking to Annie like that when she was here for Lauren and you weren't!"

Lauren was in the process of coming down the stairs when she heard Jake's comment. *"Dumped? Is that how they feel; that he dumped me on them?"* Lauren ran back to her room and slammed the door.

Annie saw Lauren at the top of the stairs and knew that she had heard the whole thing. "Lauren! Wait!" Annie called to her. "Now look what you've done! Hasn't the poor thing been through enough without this?" She went up to speak to Lauren and tried the door but it was locked. "Lauren, please unlock the door," Annie pleaded with her.

"Go away." Lauren's answer was flat and without emotion.

"Jake didn't mean what he said, it came out wrong. Please open the door." Annie tried one more time.

"Please just leave me alone," Lauren said through tears.

Annie went back downstairs. "She has locked herself in her room, the poor thing."

Caleb headed for the stairs but Will stopped him. "Leave her alone son, leave it be till morning."

"Will, this can wait. You know I believe Caleb and Lauren didn't do anything wrong. I'm going back to town but if you can talk her into coming to my office I'd appreciate it. The sooner the better," Tim said. He decided he'd let her calm down before he'd question her.

"Alright." Will showed Tim to the door. "Have a good night, Tim. At least what's left of it."

"Thanks, good night all."

Will watched as Tim rode off. When he closed the door he faced a room of solemn faces. "Boys, stable the horses. There's nothing we can do about this tonight. Caleb, you owe Annie an apology."

Caleb knew his pa was right and sought out Annie. She was in her room sitting in her rocker. Her bible was opened on her lap. Caleb tapped on the door frame.

"Come in lad." She didn't look up from her bible.

"Annie, I was way out of line and I'm sorry. Will you forgive me?"

"Aye, I already have," she answered. She continued to look at the pages but Caleb doubted she was reading. "You're going to lose her you know," Annie told him.

Lose her! She was his wife! He wanted to tell them this time and time again but promised Lauren he wouldn't! He knew she wanted to go back to Cape Jennings at the end of their agreement. If he told his pa about their marriage he wouldn't allow an annulment. He believed in *till death do you part*. Caleb wasn't going to force Lauren to stay with him when he knew she wanted to leave.

"She's not mine to lose," he said before he left the room.

****

Lauren knelt on the floor next to her bed and let the tears flow freely. She never thought she was a burden to them but after overhearing the conversation she was beside herself with grief. The hurt she felt was the same way she felt after the loss of her parents.

"Lord; show me what to do. I know this is a closed door but I don't know where you want me to go. Please prepare me for leaving them. I love all of them as if they were my family. I now understand why Caleb spent so much time away. He's in love with someone else and he didn't want to give me false hopes. Help me, Lord to sever the ties with them. I know that what you have planned for me in the future will heal the hurt I feel today. Please, show me soon, Lord. Bless this family, Lord. They have showed me so much love. But now, I am so confused. Amen."

Lauren sat in the quiet of her room contemplating what she thought God wanted her to do. Her thoughts wandered back over the day and couldn't believe that it was ruined so quickly. She leaned her aching head against the mattress and closed her eyes. The memory of Pierce's hands and mouth on her gave her cold chills. "Forgive him Father - and the town."

Chapter Thirteen

The next morning there was a grave mood at the breakfast table.

Annie and Jake were dressed for church. Annie was hoping Lauren would go with her but doubted she'd see her before she left.

Caleb was helping Annie with her chair. He froze when Lauren came down the stairs. She was wearing one of the hand-me-down dresses Sally Ann had given her. Her hair hung loose down her back. All eyes were on her as she approached the table. Her cheek was bruised and swollen where Pierce had hit her.

The blood of every Whitworth boiled in their veins when they saw the dark mark.

Caleb's knuckles turned white as he tried to control the anger he felt. He pulled a chair out for her next to his seat hoping she'd sit next to him.

"Thank you, Caleb, but I'm not going to eat." She looked tired and her eyes were red from tears she had shed throughout the night. "Mr. Whitworth, I want to thank you for sharing your home with me and showing kindness beyond measure, but I think it's time for me to go home." Will started to say something but Lauren held her hand up to stop him. "Please, sir, let me finish." She looked at Ethan. "I promised I'd help you study for your exam and

I will not leave until that is done, if it's okay with your father."

Ethan and Will exchanged looks. Lauren didn't know Ethan hadn't told his pa about the plans they had made for taking the exam. The look between the two went unnoticed as Lauren continued.

"I am going to take my chances and go back to Cape Jennings. There's a family there that will help me if I need it. I will be coming into some money in a few months so I should be fine. Annie, if you don't mind, I really don't feel up to going to church with you this morning. I hope you understand."

Annie was trying to fight the tears and swallowed hard. "Aye lass, I do. I'll be pray'n for ya," she managed to whisper.

"Lauren, can I see you alone?" Will asked. He held out his hand toward the direction of his office. "Please?"

She nodded her head and they went behind closed doors.

Caleb looked at each one around the table. No one said anything. The tension was so thick it could be cut with a knife.

"I'm sorry," he told everyone before he left the house.

"Have a seat." Will said pointing to a leather chairs.

Lauren looked around the small room that served as Will's office. There was a bookcase against the wall behind his desk filled with leather bound ledgers. His chair and desk matched the two plump leather guest chairs. She sat on the edge of the seat waiting to hear what he had to say.

Will pulled an envelope from the top drawer and held it in his hand. "I hope you will forgive me for the purpose of this correspondence but it was before I got to know you. I sent a wire to the sheriff of Cape Jennings requiring on your behalf when you first arrived. This is what I received from, a Mr. Hobbs." He handed the letter to Lauren.

"How do you know Mr. Hobbs?" Lauren asked confused.

"It's in the letter," Will answered.

She took the letter from the envelope and proceeded to read it.

Will watched her blue eyes move back and forth taking in what was on the paper. He knew when she read the part about her being penniless. Her face turned white and her hand started to tremble.

"You don't have to leave Lauren. You are part of our family. You are welcome to stay here with us." Will was trying to comfort her but his words fell on deaf ears.

"He had to sell everything? There is nothing left?" She sat staring at the letter not able to fully comprehend what she had just read. She finally looked at Will but couldn't say anything.

"Lauren, I mean it when I say you can stay here."

She nodded her head and without a word she left the room. She left the house and walked down the path to the creek. She didn't even notice Caleb sitting on the porch as she walked past him.

He could see she was upset and wondered what his pa had told her so he followed her.

141

She was sitting under the tree where she and Ethan planned his tutoring re-reading the letter when Caleb made his presence known. The look on her face alarmed him.

"What is it, Lauren?" he asked. She handed him the letter.

He sat down next to her and read its contents. He searched her face. She just stared at the creek.

"He had to sell everything, even the *Lady Lauren* and *Amanda Louise*," she told him.

"The ships?"

She nodded her head and started to cry. The full meaning of the letter finally hit her.

Caleb pulled her into his arms and held her tight as she sobbed uncontrollably. His heart ached for her pain. He wished she'd let him take care of her. He let her cry until there were no more tears to be shed. He continued to hold her as long as she'd let him. She stopped hiccupping as she calmed. Her breathing evened. He looked into her face and found her asleep. He leaned against the tree and let her sleep in his arms; his heart was breaking knowing that he'd soon have to let her go.

****

Will left his office in time to see Ethan heading for the front door. "Not so fast."

Ethan stopped and faced him. *"This is it,"* he thought to himself. "Yes sir?"

"What was Lauren talking about studying with you? What have you done?"

"I ordered the study book Pa; I got it the other day when we were in town." He quickly continued before Will could say anything. "I really want this; please let me at least take the exam to see if I can be accepted into school. If I don't pass I won't bring it up again."

"And if you do pass?" Will asked.

"Let me go." Ethan stood face to face with his father.

Will examined his son for a minute. He was no longer a child but a young man - a young man who had a dream like he did at his age. "Alright." Ethan stood staring at his pa wondering if he had heard him correctly. Will tried his best to hide his smile. The look on Ethan's face was priceless. "When is the test?"

"The end of August, I'm not sure of the exact date yet, there's a letter with the book with all the information. I'll have to go to Ellington to take it. I'll know that day or the next if I pass and if I do; school starts the first week in September."

"This doesn't give you much time to study."

"No sir, it doesn't, but Lauren said she'd help me." His heart started to race. He couldn't believe the change in his pa's attitude.

"I suggest you get going on that book," Will told him.

"Yes sir!" He hugged Will. "Pa, what made you change your mind?"

"I don't want to lose you."
It was a simple answer but one that meant the world to Ethan.

He hugged Will one more time then went to find Lauren in hopes that the good news would cheer her up. He knew she liked to sit by the creek and headed that way. He came upon Caleb leaning against the tree with Lauren

143

sound asleep in his arms. He didn't want to disturb them so he quietly turned from the couple. His heart jumped with joy from what he had seen. It looked like his brother finally came to his senses. He hoped Caleb told her he loved her and that she'd stay.

****

Lauren woke in Caleb's arms. For a brief moment she couldn't remember where she was. Memories of the night she slept next to him under the wagon came flooding back. She wanted to stay in the safety of his arms but she was hot and sweaty; then there was Cynthia to consider. It wasn't right to be sleeping in the arms of a man that belonged to someone else; even if she was married to him.

She wasn't sure how long they had been here. She knew she should get back to the house to start lunch for Annie. Caleb was still sleeping. She slowly moved out from under his arm. He stirred but he didn't wake. She went to the creek to splash cool water on her face. Her reflection confirmed how tired she had felt. The dark bruise on her cheek reminded her of the horrible incident the night before. She plunged her hands in the water to try and erase the thoughts of Pierce Compton.

Her hair hung around her shoulders adding to the heat. She twisted it in a knot then sprinkled water on the back of her neck. What she really wanted to do was take her shoes off and walk in the cool running water but time wouldn't allow it.

With a sigh of regret, she turned to return to the house when she realized Caleb had been watching her every move.

"I need to get lunch started," she said. She tried to walk past him but he gently grabbed her by the hand from where he sat. He turned her to face him. He stood up and placed his hand on either side of her face. He stroked the bruise on her cheek then kissed it. The unexpected act of compassion caused her heart to start racing.

"This isn't right!" She panicked and tried to leave but he held her there and made her look at him.

"I'm so sorry I haven't been here for you Lauren," he said. "I need to know that you forgive me and you'll let me take care of you as I promised I would."

She knew he meant every word and it broke her heart knowing he belonged to someone else. "I'm not your responsibility, Caleb." Her answer was broken as she tried to steady her breathing. "I will be leaving soon. Everyone can go back to their way of life before I came. Don't make this any harder on me then it already is!" Tears came to her eyes. She turned her head to hide them.

He pulled her close and kissed her on the lips tasting the salty tears as they escaped down her cheeks. He didn't feel her resist so he tried to hold her tighter but she pushed against his chest and stepped back.

"Don't," she told him firmly, "don't ever do that again." She walked back to the house leaving him feeling defeated.

Lauren was in the kitchen preparing sandwiches for lunch when Ethan walked in and gave her a big hug.

"He said *yes* Lauren! Pa said *yes!*" he said as he laughed.

It took her a second to realize what he was talking about. When she figured it out, she threw her arms around him in her excitement.

It was at that moment Caleb was about to enter the kitchen to see if he could try and reason with Lauren. He stopped when he saw the two embracing. He quickly stepped away before either of them noticed him. He wasn't sure what to think about what he had just witnessed. Should he stay or go? Wasn't Ethan with Samantha at the picnic? If so, what was going on between him and Lauren? He tried not to jump to any conclusions and waited out of sight.

"That's wonderful! What caused him to change his mind?" she asked.

"He said he didn't want to lose me." He looked puzzled. "Where did he think I was going?"

"It doesn't matter. All we need now is the curriculum. How long do you think it'll take for your book to get here? We really don't have much time," Lauren reminded him.

"I got it Saturday; Samantha held it for me so pa wouldn't see it until I had the chance to talk to him, which was just awhile ago."

"Oh Ethan!" She held her hand to her mouth. "I thought you already talked to him when I told you this morning that I'd help you study. I am so sorry!"

"Don't be!" he laughed. "Because of you I had the courage to face him and it worked out great!" He hugged her again and thought about how lucky Caleb was to have her. He wondered if Caleb was going to marry her. He blurted his question before he could stop himself. "How are you and Caleb getting along? Did you talk things out?" He didn't want Lauren to leave. He was hoping that what he saw by the creek was a good sign.

Caleb leaned closer to the door to hear her answer. He too wondered.

"What do you mean?" she asked trying not to show how uncomfortable it had made her.

"I was looking for you earlier. I went to the creek where you like to sit," he hesitated for a moment a little embarrassed, "and I saw you and Caleb – sleeping."

Lauren didn't know what to say at first knowing how it must have looked.

"Ethan, I shouldn't have allowed that to happen. Your brother is a gentleman and always has been. I was upset and he came to see if I was okay. I was crying and because I didn't get much rest last night I cried myself to sleep. Please, don't read anything more in what you saw. I have to leave Ethan, I need to get on with my life and leave you all to do the same."

Ethan was disappointed in her answer but not as much as the man who stood outside the door.

Chapter Fourteen

By the time mid August approached, Lauren and Ethan had studied most of the lessons. He only had two weeks before the test. Everyone settled back to a normal routine.

Lauren no longer had the spark that lit up the room when she entered. Her depression had Annie concerned. She tried to get Lauren to attend Wednesday bible study and church with her but Lauren didn't want to go back to town. Sally Ann came out to spend time with her but other than that Lauren severed all ties with the town. She was hurt by the accusations and even though she prayed about it nightly, she didn't want to face the hateful stares like the ones she received the day of the picnic.

Pierce Compton confessed to Sheriff Poynter that he was drunk and he was *mistaken* about the events that had taken place the night of the dance. He sent Lauren a written apology for his inappropriate behavior. What Lauren didn't know was that Will went to the bank and threatened to take his business to the neighboring town if he didn't set matters straight.

One night after dinner Evan found Annie on the porch enjoying the cool evening air.

"I want to do something for Lauren. She needs to be cheered up," he told her.

"What'cha got in mind lad?" He had her complete attention.

"I have to get with pa to see if he's okay with my idea and if he agrees, it'll be a lot of fun!" His eyes lit up like they did when he was a boy getting into mischief.

Ethan and Caleb were coming from the barn and saw the two with their heads together, obviously planning something.

"Okay you two, what's going on?" Ethan asked. Both schemers jumped and started to laugh.

"Come here, we need your help with this." Evan motioned for them to join them. He filled his brothers in on their plans and handed out assignments to each one. He would let either Jake or Caleb approach pa with his idea and hoped he'd go along with them. When the whispering was done and the plans made, Annie prayed over the idea. This was the first time the boys heard her pray over something other than dinner or an illness. The thought struck them as odd but if it would help they welcomed it.

****

"Lauren!" Annie yelled from the bottom of the stairs. "Are you up lass?"

It was a beautiful Saturday morning. Lauren was spending a few extra moments with the Lord when she heard Annie's call. She was up

149

and dressed ready for whatever Annie had planned for her that day.

"I'm up, is everything okay?" she asked sensing a little urgency in Annie's voice.

"Yes, yes, everything's fine but I be need'n some of your help with a few things. I have baskets of food I need to take to the neighbors, Mrs. Lose's been ill and I thought I'd bring her some meals. Can you help me?" She had no doubt Lauren would agree. As Lauren started down the stairs Annie noticed the work dress she was wearing. "You might want to change your dress, maybe the pretty violet one; it will be cooler for the ride over."

"Are you sure?" Lauren looked at the dress she was wearing and thought it would be appropriate.

"Oh, I'm sure." Annie's answer made Lauren a little suspicious but thought better then to question her.

"Alright, I'll be down in a minute." She ran back up the stairs to make Annie happy.

"And maybe the wee white ribbon to tie your hair back!" Annie shouted after her.

Now Lauren knew something was up but decided not to let Annie know she suspected anything. She looked like she was having fun and Lauren didn't want to spoil it for her.

She changed into the dress Annie suggested then went to help her load the food in the buggy. When she went outside Annie was in the wagon waiting for her. A tarp was stretched across the items in the back hiding them from Lauren's view.

"Ready to go?" Caleb asked as he exited the house. He was smiling at her.

Lauren noticed he was dressed in leisure clothes not his regular range attire. "Are you going with us?" she asked.

"If it's okay with you," he answered.

Without waiting for her to answer he ushered her to the wagon and helped her. He then jumped up and sat on the bench next to her. It was snug with the three of them. Lauren felt his muscular arm through his sleeve as she was forced to lean against him. She turned to survey the back of the wagon to get her mind off of him.

"What's all this under the tarp?" she asked. "Are we feeding an army?"

Caleb looked at her with his handsome smile and winked but didn't answer her. Now she definitely knew something was brewing which made her a little nervous.

"Where did you say this neighbor lived?" she asked.

"We'll be there in about fifteen minutes, not long at all," Annie told her.

This helped Lauren relax knowing they weren't going to town but she was very curious as to what they had in store for her.

Lauren was surprised at how at ease she was with Caleb sitting so close to her, especially after the incident by the creek. She dreamed about the afternoon he kissed her and wished things could be different between them. He often left the house after dinner and Lauren assumed he went to see Cynthia. The image of Cynthia's arms around him and her lips on his sent jealously through her. She constantly had to ask for forgiveness for her emotions she couldn't control.

They rounded the bend near Lake Eden when Caleb pulled the wagon from the road.

Lauren saw the horses and buggies under a shade tree. Jake and Sally Ann were the first to see them arrive and waved to them.

"What's this?" Lauren asked. She saw the Whitworth family apparently setting up for a picnic.

"We thought we all could use a wee bit of a break so we decided on a picnic! It'll probably be a long time before we can all get together if Ethan passes that test and goes off to school." Annie explained. She didn't have the heart to tell Lauren that she was the reason behind the day's festivities.

Lauren thought it was a wonderful idea then wondered why she told them they were delivering food to a neighbor.

"Why did you tell me we were...." she started to ask but before she finished Annie answered her.

"Because I know you and if I told you we were take'n a day off you would've found Ethan and study, study, study! He needs a break and so do you."

"You know me too well." Lauren's face turned red from the truth.

"We invited a few friends to join us for the day. You know most of them; the Poynters, Sally Anne, Samantha and a couple other ladies and their families from the bible study group."

Lauren looked a little leery when she found out there would be people from town.

Caleb felt her stiffen and tried to assure her it would be fine. "You'll like them, I promise." He pulled the wagon along side the others and before she could blink everyone was there unloading the baskets of food, blankets, fishing poles and horseshoes.

Lauren was holding a fishing pole in her hand when Caleb approached her with his. "Do you fish Lauren?" he asked.

"No! I've seen them fish off the docks in Cape Jennings but I was never allowed. It's not lady like you know," she teased.

"Well, we'll just have to see about that!" Caleb told her.

Before she could protest, he hooked his arm in hers and led her to the lake's bank. Will already had his line in the water.

"If you think you're coming over here to steal my fish you better think twice." He winked at her.

"No sir! I wouldn't dream of it since I have no clue how this all works," she said as she examined the line, hook, and pole.

"Come on, we'll move down here," Caleb said laughing. "He never catches anything anyways."

"I heard that," Will said as he leaned against the willow behind him. He pushed his hat over his eyes. Will was glad he agreed to join them. It felt good to be here again. He missed his wife and thought that if he came back to the lake it would make him sad but instead it brought back good memories.

Caleb found a fat, wiggly worm from the bucket of dirt and tried to hand it to Lauren.

"There is no way I'm going to touch that!" She took a step back and wrinkled her nose at it.

Caleb laughed at her and showed her how it was done then rinsed his hands in the water. "See, it's not hard. But, for luck you have to kiss it." The look on Lauren's face made him laugh. "I'm kidding!" He said to her and tossed her line in the water. "Sit here and watch for the cork to be pulled under, and then tug the pole to set the hook."

She looked at him like he was speaking another language. He laughed at the blank stare she gave him. "I'll tell you what, I'll sit here with you and help you the first time."

"And steal my fish?" She looked up at him shading her eyes with her hand. "I don't think so, you can move down there." She pointed to a spot further down the bank.

"Territorial aren't we?" He plopped his hat on her head and started to leave then turned back to her. "By the way, the one that catches the least has to clean all the fish for supper."

She picked up a clump of dirt and threw it barely missing him. He left her to fend for herself laughing as he found a spot under a shade tree.

Lauren sat daydreaming and enjoying the laughter around her when she noticed her cork bobbing. She almost yelled for Caleb to help her but decided she'd show him she could take care of the beast by herself.

"Wait for it to go under," she remembered him telling her, *"then set the hook."*

She watched the cork bob a few more times then it went under. With all her might, she tried to set the hook thinking there was a fat fish on the end of the line. The line was empty and made the pole lighter then she thought. She didn't hear Jake and Sally Ann behind her and her pole smacked Jake right between his eyes knocking off his hat.

Sally Ann couldn't contain her laughter when she saw the startled look on Jake's and Lauren's faces.

"Jake! Are you? I'm so sorry!" Lauren saw the red welt on his forehead and felt awful.

Caleb and Will came over to see if he was okay. Seeing no real harm had been done, they too couldn't help but laugh at the scene.

"I don't know about you Caleb but I think Lauren is the winner, she got the biggest catch!" Will told him and took the fishing pole from Lauren. "I think you've done enough damage for the day." He headed back to his spot in the shade still laughing.

"Jake, I'm so sorry, are you sure you're okay?" Lauren's concerned look melted his heart and he gave her a big hug.

"I'll survive," he reassured her. "Why don't we try horseshoes? You and Caleb against me and Sally Ann?'

"I have a better idea," Sally Ann said still laughing, "Lauren and I against the two of you. The losers have to jump in the lake."

The Whitworth men looked at each other then grinned.

"Let the game begin," Jake said with a mischievous smile.

Lauren grabbed Sally Ann by the arm and pulled her back. "I don't know how to play. What if I kill someone?" She giggled as she tried to look serious.

"If you haven't noticed by now, the Whitworth's have hard heads. You can't do much damage to them," she answered.

Lauren caught on quickly and the women won two out of three matches.

"This way gents!" Sally Ann motioned toward the lake. "Be thankful it's a very warm day."

With defeated looks on their faces the men headed toward the lake. When they arrived, they took off their shoes, socks and shirts.

Ethan, Evan and Samantha caught wind of the contest and were there to support the winners as they yelled and clapped. Before Lauren and Sally Ann realized what they had planned, Caleb and Jake picked them up and jumped in the lake with them screaming.

Lauren stood up sputtering. She threw a handful of water in Caleb's face. She tried to exit the lake but kept slipping on the slick bottom.

"You really didn't think you won did you?" Caleb whispered in her ear. He grabbed her arm to help her out of the water.

His devilish grin was more than she could handle. She enjoyed being close to him and it frightened her. She knew she had to move away.

"You're a rat Caleb Whitworth! A big, fat, wet rat!" She splashed water at him to prove her point and lost her footing. The weight of her wet dress pulled her under the water.

Caleb waited until she found her footing then helped her get out of the water. By now there was a crowd by the lake enjoying the unexpected entertainment. They were so involved with getting them out of the water; no one noticed the buggy approaching with a lone passenger.

Samantha helped Sally Ann and Lauren wring out their wet dresses when she noticed Cynthia pulling in to join the picnic. She was dressed in a white blouse and light blue skirt with a wide brimmed hat to shade her face from the sun.

"Who invited her?" Samantha asked.

Sally Ann and Lauren looked to see who she was referring to.

"Caleb." Lauren's answer was short and full of hurt.

Samantha and Sally Ann exchanged looks, feeling Lauren's pain.

"Why would he invite her?" Samantha asked.

"I don't know but let's not let it spoil the day. I've had so much fun and I don't want it to end." Lauren didn't want her jealousy to ruin their fun so she tried to act like it didn't bother her. She squeezed Samantha's hand. "Let's help Annie get lunch together. I'm starving!"

Cynthia approached Annie and the other ladies as they spread out blankets and inspected the goods in each basket.

"Here's another one for your banquet. Oh my, look at all this food! It's wonderful!" Cynthia said. She set her basket down and smiled at the ladies. She looked up and saw the wet women coming toward them. She recognized Caleb's hat on Lauren and her blood began to boil. "What happened to them?" she asked in disgust.

"Jake and Caleb jumped in the lake with them," Mrs. Poynter said while laughing. "You should have seen the look on the girls' faces! It was priceless!"

The thought of Caleb with Lauren in his arms angered Cynthia even more. In her mind he belonged to her and she didn't want another woman near him. She worked too hard to get his attention and she wasn't going to let some stranger come in and undo everything.

"Annie!" Lauren ran up to her and hugged her making her squeal when Lauren got her wet. "What can we do to help?

"Get me a change of clothes for one you little varmint!" She smacked Lauren lovingly then handed out instructions to the girls.

Annie watched Lauren's face when she saw Cynthia wander toward the game of horseshoes. She didn't know who invited her but she was sure to give them a tongue lashing when she found out. She tried to busy Lauren to keep her mind off the tall blonde.

Cynthia walked seductively toward the men when she noticed they were watching her approach. She thought Caleb looked extremely handsome with his shirt half unbuttoned, water dripping from wet curls, and his bare feet. His white teeth stood out against his tanned face as he laughed. She remembered him looking like that when they were younger. The boys would sneak away from school during lunch and swim in a near by pond. The girls would hide and watch them;

giggling as they made plans as to which one they were going to marry when they got older. She made it quite clear back then that no one was to touch her Caleb.

She walked right up to Caleb ignoring the other men and possessively grabbed his arm.

"Lunch is ready, I was sent down here to get all of you," she lied. "Look at you Caleb, you're a mess. Here let me..." She started to smooth out his hair but he grabbed her hand.

"I'm fine," he said as he smiled politely at her. "I'll probably go back in the water after lunch, so you don't need to bother with it." He wasn't blind to her games and made sure he didn't lead her on in anyway.

"Hello Cynthia, what brings you out here?" Jake asked her.

"I heard you talking about the picnic with Sally Ann and Samantha this morning when you picked them up." She stuck out her bottom lip as if she had been deeply hurt. "I was surprised you forgot to invite me, we've been friends for so long." She looked up at Caleb with her most charming smile. "I knew you wouldn't mind if I tagged along."

"Oh! If you only knew!" Caleb thought to himself but his pa taught him to always be a gentleman so he just smiled. "You know you're welcome," he assured her.

"Shall we eat lunch?" She hooked her arm in Caleb's and pulled him toward the group gathering for the meal.

Cynthia laughed and chattered during lunch making sure Lauren could hear her.

Lauren kept herself busy to keep her attention off of them. She tried not to watch but once in awhile she'd look in their direction and it hurt to see them together. Caleb was always the gentleman giving her his complete attention when she asked him a question.   Lauren could hear his deep voice as he spoke to Cynthia. She tried to tell herself she didn't care but her heart told her differently. She needed to move away from the two and find something to do.

She overheard Toby Taylor trying to convince his mamma he was old enough to fish alone but Mrs. Taylor wouldn't let him go to the lake by himself.

"If I have your permission, I'll take him," Lauren offered. "I need to master this sport, especially after what happened this morning."

Mrs. Taylor smiled at Lauren and looked relieved to get the eight year old out from under her feet.

"Are you sure?" Mrs. Taylor asked. "He can be a handful."

"What do you say Toby? Will you show me how this is done the right way?" Lauren asked the freckled face boy.

"Sure! Com'on!" He grabbed Lauren by the hand and started to run toward the lake then remembered something. He ran back to his ma and hugged her pregnant belly. "Thanks mamma!"

Lauren took his hand and looked back at his laughing ma. She mouthed *thank you* to Lauren making her laugh as well.

Mrs. Taylor was due to have her second baby soon. Lauren couldn't imagine how she'd manage if her second was as spunky as Toby.

Lauren squealed when she tried to hook her worm making Toby laugh. She finally got used to the slimy, sticky, worm and mastered the process of fishing. The two of them sat on the bank and caught one fish after another. When they had enough they grabbed their stringer to show off their accomplishment.

Caleb and Cynthia were still sitting in the shade talking when Lauren walked up to them. She plopped her stringer between the two of them causing Cynthia to scream when one started to flop on her skirt.

"Mr. Whitworth, I think you have some fish to clean." She smiled in victory and walked away from the couple.

Everyone laughed and congratulated Lauren and Toby on their catch.

"Thanks for dinner you two!" Will said rustling Toby's curls. "I guess we had to send a woman to do a man's job. Get up Caleb and get them fish cleaned. We'll eat them for supper so hurry! My mouth's watering!"

"Yes sir!" Caleb laughed as well and had to admit he had met his match. He was also thankful for the excuse to leave clingy Cynthia.

Lauren sighed as the events from such a wonderful day came to an end. She enjoyed meeting the Prewitt's and the Taylor's, especially Toby. The wagons and buggies left one at a time leaving Will, Lauren, Annie, Caleb, and Cynthia.

The men helped Annie and Lauren in the wagon then Caleb walked Cynthia to her buggy. Half way there she let out a shout of pain and gracefully collapsed on the ground holding her ankle.

"Oh, Caleb, I twisted my ankle!" she moaned as she rubbed her leg.

"Let me take a look," Caleb offered.

He lifted the hem of her dress to inspect her ankle. When he put his hand under her heel to lift her foot she let out a cry of pain.

"I don't think I can walk," she moaned.

Without a word he lifted her in his arms and put her in the buggy. He made his way back to the wagon to let them know what had happened. "I need to take Cynthia back to town, she twisted her ankle."

"So we heard," Annie snapped.

Before he had a chance to move away from the wagon she slapped the reins and the team bolted forward. Caleb had to jump back so it wouldn't run over his feet.

Shaking his head, Will gave him a sorrowful look then followed the wagon.

Caleb went back to the buggy and tied his horse to the back and climbed in next to Cynthia.

"Thank you, Caleb for helping me. I don't know what I would have done if you had already left," she purred.

"No problem," he said between clenched teeth.

She held his arm and rested her head on his shoulder. They caught up to the wagon before it reached the road.

Cynthia made sure Lauren saw her head on Caleb's shoulder then gave her a sweet smile before waving her good bye.

"That woman," Annie spat. "One of these days her games are going to hurt someone. She's evil I tell ya, just evil."

Lauren didn't comment. Her broken heart told her that Cynthia's games already did their damage.

Cynthia snuggled against Caleb to the point he started to feel very uncomfortable. Her non-stop chatter was giving him a headache. It was almost dark when he pulled up in front of the boarding house where she stayed.

"I'll take the buggy back to the livery for you," he offered. He started to get out buggy but she pulled him back to his seat.

"Caleb, you don't have to leave so soon. Stay and talk with me. I get so lonely here." She looked up at him with pleading eyes.

"I can't," he told her.

She wouldn't believe his refusal so she tried again. This time she leaned against him and pulled his face toward hers. "Yes, you can, there's no one waiting for you at home." She kissed him on the mouth.

He pushed her as far away as the buggy seat would allow. "Cynthia! This has got to stop! If I led you to believe that there is anything between us other then friendship I'm sorry. I don't feel the way you want me to toward you."

Her pleading eyes gave way to anger. She slapped him across the face as hard as she could. "I have waited for you Caleb since we were children. I saved myself for you and only you. I can't believe you can sit here and tell me you don't feel the same way!" Before he could say anything she gathered her skirt and hopped out of the buggy. "You're wrong about us," she hissed, "you'll see."

Caleb rubbed his face where she had slapped him. He marveled at how her ankle healed so quickly. She stomped up the walkway without the slightest limp. He waited until she was safe inside the house before returning the buggy to the livery.

He wondered what Lauren was doing. It never occurred to him until then that he thought of her often. He wished he could dismiss her as easily as she did him. She'd be leaving soon and when she was gone he hoped he could concentrate on getting his life back to normal, if he could remember what that was like before she entered it.

****

Lauren helped clean out the wagon when they returned home then went to her room. She sat and brushed her dark hair until it was tangle free then slipped into her night gown. She tried to pray but visions of Caleb and Cynthia kept running through her mind.

"Thank you, for such a beautiful day. Lord, please help me to forget about Caleb. I love him but he belongs to someone else. I need you to help me stay strong so that I can move on. Forgive me where I fail you."

She thought back on some of the events from the picnic and smiled when she remembered Cynthia scream because the fish flopped on her. "Forgive me, for being mean to Cynthia, I pray her and Caleb will be happy together."

Lauren tried to sleep but her mind wouldn't stop replaying the scenes with Caleb and Cynthia. She decided it was time to write to Mr. Hobbs and make arrangements for her to return to Cape Jennings, regardless of the danger.

August 13, 1884

Dearest Mr. and Mrs. Hobbs,

I am writing to ask if your offer for lodging is still available. Mr. Whitworth allowed me to read the letter you sent him since it concerned my finances. Many events have taken place which will not allow me to stay with the Whitworth's any longer. I know that my request will cause you confusion and concern but please, be assured that I am fine and the Whitworth's have been the most gracious family, but I can no longer impose on their kindness. I know you are wondering about my husband and I will explain our relationship in detail when I see you. I need to stay until the first of September to fulfill a promise to one of the younger Whitworth's.

If your offer still stands, please write to me. Thank you, so much for your love and help with my uncle's debts. I will pay you back for your generosity; how I don't know but I know the Lord will help me find a way.

In Christ,

Lauren Bailey

She sealed and addressed the letter before crawling back to bed. She felt as if a huge burden had been lifted from her. She soon drifted off to sleep.

After a sleepless night she sought after anyone who might be going to town the next day. She found Will in his office going over paperwork.

"Good morning, are you going to town in the morning?" she asked him.

"Yes, I am. Can I get something for you?"

"Would you mind posting this for me?" Lauren gave her letter to Will.

He noticed the address and sadness filled his heart. "My offer still stands, you are welcome to stay."

"I appreciate it, but it is time for me to go home. By the time the travel arrangements are made and Ethan's test has been taken, I will be of age."

"Very well, then." He took the letter and placed in his desk drawer. He hoped by some miracle the letter would disappear by the next morning. But when he collected his mail to take to town it was still in the drawer. Regretfully, he added it to his pile and headed to town with a heavy heart.

Chapter Fifteen

"Concentrate Ethan, I know you know the answer to this one." Lauren was trying desperately to keep Ethan's attention on his studies but he was miles away. They only had a week before he took the test. She could feel his anxiety and closed the book and set it on the ground next to her.

"What are you doing?" Ethan asked her.

"There's something bothering you. Do you want to talk?" She hoped that this would ease his mind a little.

"I guess I'm nervous. What if I don't do well? All this studying would be for nothing." He pulled at a piece of grass and fiddle with it.

"Do you want this Ethan Whitworth?" Lauren asked him.

"More than anything," he answered.

"In the book of John in the bible, God tells us that if we abide, or stay, in Him and stay in His word, all we need to do is ask for our heart's desire and He will give it to us. *'If ye abide in me, and my words abide in you, ye shall ask what ye will, and it shall be done unto you',*" Lauren quoted. She watched as he thought on what she had said. "I believe in His promises and I've been praying for you."

"How do you know this? How do you know that God even hears what you ask of Him?" he asked with questioning eyes.

"You need to believe in who He is and have faith," she told him.

"How?"

Lauren felt the Holy Spirit move as she explained the plan of salvation to him.

"It's very simple. All you need to do is accept Christ as the son of God, His only son, and that He came to earth to save us from our sins. You see, we all have sinned and no matter how good we try to be its never good enough; that's why God sent Jesus. He was the perfect sacrifice for our sins." She sat quietly as she let him to digest what she had explained. She prayed silently that God would continue to give her the words she needed.

He nodded his head to let her know he understood what she had told him.

"Is this something you would like to do Ethan? Would you like to ask Jesus into your heart and become one of His children?"

"Yes, I would."

She took his hands into hers and they prayed together. She helped him in prayer and when they were done Ethan didn't lift his head for a moment. When he did Lauren saw the tears that were on his cheeks. She cried with him and they held each other as they celebrated his decision.

He let out a deep breath and smiled. "I feel like the world has been lifted off of me. It's such peace."

"Yes, it is. You need to get a bible and read to learn more about Jesus. This will help you learn how to lean on Him."

"Thank you, Lauren." Ethan hugged her again. "I love you so much."

Lauren let the tears flow when he told her that he loved her. She knew that the love he had for her was that of a brother's. He held her tighter. "I'm sorry you have to leave, I wish you would stay," he whispered.

She pulled away and wiped the tears from her face. "I have to leave. But I won't be leaving until you are settled in school!"

"Good!" he said. "Let's get back to the book."

They went back to the quizzing but this time it was Lauren who couldn't concentrate. She wanted to run to the house and tell Annie that Ethan was a new believer.

****

Annie had asked Caleb to let Lauren and Ethan know supper was ready. He headed toward the creek. He spent the past few days on the range and he hoped that in his absence Lauren would have missed him. He was at the edge of the path when he stopped short at the sight of Lauren and Ethan holding each other. Further shock set in when he heard Ethan tell her that he loved her. All his hopes crashed around him. He left the two without a word and went to the barn. He saddled his horse and rode off leaving Evan standing in the yard.

"Caleb!" Evan shouted, but Caleb was too far away to hear him. He saw the anger on his brother's face and wondered what had happened.

"Where's he off to in such a hurry?" Jake asked.

"Don't know, I came out to see if he got Lauren and Ethan and he just took off like a bat out'a.." he snapped his mouth shut when he saw Lauren approach.

"Something's wrong, he was angry," Jake said.

"Who's angry?" Ethan asked.

"Caleb, he just took off madder than a hornet," Evan told them. "Oh well, more fried chicken for me."

Jake smacked him on the back of the head. "That's all you think about is your stomach. Come on, Annie's waiting for us."

"Where's Caleb?" Will asked after everyone was seated for dinner.

"He left," Evan told him.

"Did he say where he was going?"

"No sir," Evan told him then stuffed a hot roll in his mouth. "But he was pretty mad."

"Pa, I was wondering what you and Annie think about Lauren going with me to Ellington. I could use the company and she can help me study before the test," Ethan mentioned trying to change the subject.

"Not chaperoned?" Annie asked shocked. "Out of the question; how would that look?"

"Well, Samantha is going to ask her pa if she can go, too. We were hoping Lauren could be the chaperone, if that's okay with you?" He asked Lauren.

"I don't mind, if your father is alright with it. But, I'm sure you won't get much studying done with such a pretty young lady nearby," Lauren teased.

"Probably not but I'll feel better having someone from home there with me," he confessed.

"I'll have Jake go with you," Will told them.

"Sorry Pa, I can't. I promised to help Sally Ann with a few repairs at the café next week. You'll have to see if Caleb can do it."

"I'll see if I can find him after dinner. Do you think Samantha's pa will let her go?" Will asked Ethan.

"If we have proper chaperones he will, I'm sure of it."

"I'll see to Caleb then I'm going to check with Mr. Colby. I want to hear for myself that he's okay with Samantha going," Will said.

"Is Ellington a big town?" Lauren asked.

"It's more like a city really, not a big one but it has a lot more to offer. I think you'l like it when you get there. They actually have brick walkways and gas lamps to light the streets." Jake told her.

Ethan and Lauren's eyes lit up at the idea of going to a city.

"Count me in!" Evan said.

"You'll be fine right here son," Will laughed.

"Aw! Pa! That's not fair!" He pouted.

"That will be enough," Will warned.

Everyone laughed at Evan when he stuck his tongue out at Ethan. He too joined in with the laughter. He knew that one day he'd have his turn.

****

Caleb pulled back on the reins of his horse Trinket. He found himself at Lake Eden. He understood why his mother loved it there. He dismounted and sat in the cool grass. He listened to the sounds of the evening and allowed peace to fill him. The shadows grew long as the sun went behind the trees. He was hurting and didn't know how to handle it. He had never had time for romance or courting then Lauren came into his life and turned his world up side down. She was like a breath of fresh air. She managed to work her way into his heart before he realized it. He was angry at her and Ethan but then scolded himself for allowing such feelings. It wasn't their fault that they had fallen in love; Ethan was there for her while he ran and hid. His wondered about Samantha and how she fit in the picture. Ethan spent as much time with her as he could. His ponderings were interrupted when he heard a rider approach.

Will had withdrawn from the dinner conversation as he thought about Caleb. He hoped to find him after he was done eating. It wasn't like Caleb to ride off as he did. He was relieved when he didn't have look too long. "Everything okay?" Will asked him
"Yeah."
"You had us concerned taking off like that. Want to talk?" Will offered.
"No, everything's fine," he assured him.
Will didn't believe him but he wasn't going to pressure him for answers. "Good. I need you to do something for Ethan. I need you to go with him to Ellington. He wants family with him."
"Why can't Jake go?" Caleb asked.

"He has a commitment at Sally Ann's and I need to watch things at home. This is only if Samantha is allowed to go. You and Lauren will be chaperones." He watched as Caleb's face turned to stone.

"No! She can do it by herself. She'll be fine."

"You will go with them Caleb and that's final. I don't know what's gotten into you but Ethan needs you. He's always looked up to you most out of all his brothers. Don't let him down."

"Yes sir. When do we leave?" Caleb knew arguing would do him no good.

"His test is Monday. You'll be leaving on the Saturday stage."

"Saturday? Why so early? It only takes six hours to get there by stage." Caleb's anger was growing. He wanted to spend as little time as possible around them.

"The stage leaves late Saturday morning getting you to Ellington in the evening. This will give Ethan a chance to get settled before he has to take the test. Lauren will be there for any last minute studying he might want to do." Will noticed Caleb was still not happy with this and tried to make it sound fun. "You can take the girls to dinner and shopping. I don't think Samantha's ever been out of Clayton's Creek and it'll be exciting for her. Now, come home, Annie has a plate for you." Will turned his horse toward home and waited for Caleb to mount Trinket.

"Samantha's going?" Caleb asked confused.

"If her father will allow," Will answered him. He wanted to ask Caleb what was on his heart but knew he probably wouldn't share. They talked about the ranch and what needed to be done before fall.

Caleb remembered the first time he went to a big city and the excitement he had felt. He would do it for Ethan. As far as Lauren was concerned, he was determined to stay as far away from her as he possibly could.

Chapter Sixteen

The twin's eighteenth birthday was celebrated a couple days before Ethan had to leave for Ellington.

Will treated the family to dinner at Sally Ann's so Annie could spend the time with them instead of in the kitchen. They were all there except Caleb who was spending his last few days before the trip on the range.

Will was discouraged that he didn't come in; at least for the boys' birthday.

The evening was full of the usual laughter when they were together and it gave the dining area a cheerful atmosphere. Gifts were exchanged and opened at the table after Sally Ann surprise them all with a beautiful cake. Annie, Lauren, and Samantha pitched in and bought Ethan his first bible. When he opened the wrapper, there were raised eyebrows. No comments were made on what they thought was an unusual gift. As they were heading toward the door to leave, Caleb made his appearance.

"Better late then never!" Jake announced. They all laughed and were glad to see he at least made an attempt to be there.

"Sorry, I would have been here earlier but we had calving problems," he explained.

"How did it go? Did we lose the calf?" Will asked.

"No, they're fine," Caleb answered.

"Good! Let's go home," Will said as he pat Caleb on the back. "You need to stay home for the next couple of days. Kent can handle anything that might go wrong. If there are problems he can send for help."

Caleb knew that wasn't a suggestion but another order so he didn't argue. He was tired and it would be nice to sleep in a bed a couple nights before the bumpy stage ride to Ellington.

They headed for home unaware of the cold, hateful eyes watching the family as they left for Eden.

Cynthia Redding didn't like it when she didn't get what she wanted. She despised Lauren and how the Whitworth's treated her like one of the family. The hatred grew everyday as she vowed she'd get rid of her one way or another. She knew that Lauren was the wall that stood between her and Caleb; a wall that needed to be removed so that she could have him to herself.

She grew up with a drunk for a father in a one room shack outside of town. Her mother left them when she was a young child. After her father finally drank himself to death, she moved to town as a teen taking whatever jobs she could to pay for her room and board. Her beauty didn't go unnoticed and she had plenty of marriage proposals but her heart was set on Caleb. She hated her life and knew that marrying him would be her ticket to freedom. She wasn't going to let anything or anyone stop her from making her lifetime dream a reality; no matter the cost.

****

The days flew by and before they knew it the family was back in town waiting for the stage to leave for Ellington.

Mr. Colby was there to wish his daughter a safe trip. "Caleb, may speak to you?" Mr. Colby asked.

"Sir?"

"You take care of my little girl, you hear? She's all I have since her ma died."

"Yes sir."

"Here," he handed Caleb some money, "she might want to purchase something."

"We'll take care of her, I promise," Caleb assured him as he slipped the money in his pocket.

"You come to the ranch for dinner while she's gone. We'll keep your mind off of her absence," Annie offered.

"I just might do that, Annie. Thank you."

Lauren felt Samantha's apprehension about leaving. "Are you scared?" she asked her.

"A little. I've never been away from papa before and I'm worried about him. I hope he eats while I'm gone. The accounts! He'll need to balance them every day." The wheels were starting to turn in her pretty head. Lauren laughed at her. "Maybe I shouldn't go," Samantha said.

"Are you kidding? You're going to have a great time. Annie promised to take care of feeding your pa and if he forgets. If he forgets the books you can be balanced them when you get back. We're only going to be gone a few days," Lauren reminded her.

Samantha realized she was over reacting and started to giggle.

"Load up folks!" the stage driver yelled.

"This is it," Lauren told Samantha. "Go give your pa a hug and don't let him see you worrying." Lauren gave her a little nudge in Mr. Colby's direction. Lauren watched as Annie hugged everyone. She had tears in her eyes. "My goodness Annie! What's this all about?" Lauren asked laughing.

Annie sniffed and blew her nose in her hanky. "My boys are all grown up." she said. "They won't be need'n me much longer."

"Annie!" Will called, "did you pack Ethan's suit?"

She laughed and looked at Lauren. "I guess maybe I still have a few years with them." They both laughed and Annie assured Will that Ethan was ready to go.

"It's time to board," Caleb told Lauren.

She didn't notice him standing so close to her. When he spoke it made her jump. "Oh! Okay. Samantha, are you ready?"

"Yes!" she answered with excitement.

Caleb helped Lauren, Samantha, and another woman who would be traveling to the next town in the stage. Before he could board, a short man in business attire rudely pushed his way through the door.

Caleb turned to look at Ethan to see if he witnessed such bravery.

"Must be in a hurry," Ethan whispered to Caleb.

All the women were seated on one side of the stage. It didn't take long before Caleb realized the business man's intentions. He plopped himself down across from Lauren. Not wasting any time in his introductions.

"Edward Sneed at your service." He tipped his hat at the ladies. "If I can be of any service to you on this trip please don't hesitate to ask. I understand you'll be going as far as Ellington? That's wonderful! So am I! I hope you won't think it too bold if I ask where you will be staying."

"Thank you, sir. We will be..." Samantha started to answer Sneed.

Lauren quickly picked up on his intentions and interrupted her. "That is very generous but we're not traveling alone. My friend made the arrangements so we don't know where we will be lodging," she politely answered him.

Caleb pushed his large form in the stage with Ethan following. He made a point to make this man uncomfortable. He sat as close as he could leaving the stranger little room to move, let alone breathe.

"Sir! Do you mind? This is a very expensive suite and you're going to wrinkle it!" He nudged at Caleb's muscular form but Caleb didn't budge.

"Miss Bailey, would you mind switching seats with this gentleman? You are smaller and it would give us more room on this side." Caleb always used her first name when he spoke to her. His cold behavior was starting to irritate her but she thought two could play his game.

"Samantha is smaller; I think it would be better if she sat there."

Before he had a chance to say another word Lauren helped Samantha and Mr. Sneed maneuver to their new seats.

Caleb didn't say a word. Lauren knew he was mad when she saw his cheek muscle twitch with anger.

When the driver was satisfied everyone was situated, he climbed on the stage and shouted to the team.

Ethan and Samantha waved out the windows ignorant to the storm that was building within the stage.

Lauren was determined to enjoy herself so she ignored Caleb's behavior. She spoke to Mr. Sneed and the elderly woman next to her. The road was dry and hard causing the ride to be very bumpy. Lauren felt like she was once again in the back of Caleb's wagon.

It wasn't long before they were at their first stop and the older woman departed leaving more room for them during the remainder of the trip. They had five minutes to stretch their legs and see to other needs before continuing their journey. When it was time to leave, Caleb pulled Lauren back by the arm and let Mr. Sneed and the others get on the stage first. He climbed in before Lauren and then turned to give her a hand. Mr. Sneed was seated alone by the window so Caleb plopped down and pulled Lauren in the seat next to him. He was now between her and Sneed. His actions were more then Lauren could handle and it was her turn to be angry. She wasn't going to let him have his way with the foolish game he was playing.

"Mr. Sneed, why don't you sit across from me so we can continue our conversation?" she asked ever so sweetly. She had to lean in front of Caleb so she could see Sneed.

"Excellent idea," he said very pleased that such a beautiful woman was giving him attention. He quickly relocated across from her.

Caleb and Lauren were miserable with each other and with Sneed. He talked non-stop. Lauren scolded herself for letting Caleb irk her so badly that now she had to pretend to be interested in what this man had to say.

It felt like six days instead of six hours before they finally arrived in Ellington. When the stage stopped at the depot, Lauren had to keep herself from jumping down on her own to get away from Caleb and Sneed. She waited patiently for Sneed to exit. Sneed extended his hand to help her out but before she could grasp it Caleb went for the door.

"Thank you, I'll take it from here," he said smiling at Sneed. He offered Lauren his hand.

She didn't take it and tried to get out on her own. Her shoe got caught on the hem of her skirt causing her to stumble. Caleb was quick to steady her and helped her to her feet.

"Miss Bailey, are you alright?" Sneed asked her in an overly concerned voice.

"Yes, thank you. Mr. Whitworth, you can let go of me now." Her face was red from embarrassment. Caleb released her arm. He helped Samantha down then he had Ethan retrieved their bags.

Lauren's anger melted when she saw the expression on Samantha's face and the wonder in her eyes. She was in awe of the street lights, two and three story brick buildings, and so many fancy carriages! Her excitement grew more when she learned they'd be riding in one to get to their hotel.

Sneed headed in Lauren's direction when Caleb intercepted him. Lauren saw Caleb say something to him then they shook hands. Sneed looked at her and tipped his hat and went on his way. When Samantha was with Ethan taking in all the sights Lauren went to Caleb, determined to know what he said to Sneed. He saw her headed his way and tried to hide the smile on his face.

"What did you say to him?" she demanded.

He could tell she was irritated by the challenging look in her eyes. "I told him you were my wife." He watched the anger cross her face as the words registered in her mind.

"You did what?" She tried to keep her voice down so Samantha and Ethan wouldn't hear her.

"It's the truth; it was poor judgment the way you were leading him on like you did." He had never seen her so furious. He thought he'd better put a safe distance between them. He left her fuming, not allowing her to say another word. He hired an open carriage so they could see the city.

The driver pointed out places of interest as they headed toward the hotel. Samantha's excitement pulled Lauren from her angry thoughts. She sat with her mouth opened when Caleb pointed to their hotel.

The *Ellington Grande* stood like a castle at the end of the street. It was a four story brick building and as long as the street. Lights burned on the balconies giving it a warm welcoming glow.

"Isn't it beautiful Lauren?" Samantha asked. "I wish papa could see this."

"Yes it is," Lauren answered. She felt Caleb's eyes on her but refused to look at him. She wasn't sure how she was going to make it through the next few days without spoiling it for Samantha and Ethan. She knew that once she was in her room she would have to go to the Lord for His advice and strength.

The carriage stopped in front of the hotel. A footman helped the women then gathered their luggage. They were dressed in black and white tuxedoes with white gloves on their hands.

Caleb secured two rooms and followed the bellman up the stairs.

Samantha had never seen anything so elaborate in her life. The floors were covered with plush carpet. Red and gold velvet drapes hung from ceiling to floor with delicate lace covering the windows. Crystal chandeliers hung from the ceilings casting sparkles on the walls from the flickering lights. Vases of fresh cut flowers were used to accent the tables along the long hallways.

The bellman opened a door and stepped back allowing the ladies to enter the elegant sitting room. It was decorated in greens and gold.

"Pinch me Lauren, I think I died and went to heaven," she whispered. Lauren laughed at her then gave her a little pinch. "Thank you, Ethan, for inviting me. This is wonderful!" Samantha hugged him making him blush.

"I'm glad your pa let you come with us." His voice cracked as he tried to answer her.

"Will an hour be enough time to get ready for dinner?" Caleb asked them.

"Yes," Lauren answered.

"We'll eat downstairs in the hotel's dining room. We'll be back to get you in an hour," Caleb told them before he and Ethan followed the bellman to their room.

Lauren knew that the dining area would be as elegant as the rest of the hotel. She had lodged in elegant hotels with her parents. Lauren helped Samantha with her hair pulling the curls back with combs and letting them cascade down her back. She pinned all of hers up away from her face allowing a few curly strands to hang loose.

Samantha thought she looked like a Greek Goddess she had seen in one of her school books. "You look beautiful, Lauren!"

"Thank you, Samantha, so do you!" Lauren watched her blush from the comment and laughed.

"Lauren, are you mad at Caleb?" Samantha had noticed the way the two were acting and knew something was wrong.

Lauren felt awful thinking she might be making the trip uncomfortable. "No. Well, yes. I was, but it'll be okay. I just need to pray about it. I'm sorry if I ruined anything for you. I want you to enjoy your trip."

"Do you want me to pray with you?" Samantha asked her.

Lauren smiled at her. "That would be nice."

They bowed their heads and spent time with the Lord. They thanked Him for the safety of their trip; ask for help with Ethan's test, and to put peace in Caleb's and Lauren's hearts.

Lauren felt a quietness fill her soul. She was glad to have Samantha with her.

A knock on the door brought them to their feet. They found Ethan dressed in his suit waiting for them outside. His mouth dropped when he saw Samantha. He mechanically held out his arm to escort her.

"Where's Caleb?" Samantha asked as she glanced down the hall.

"He didn't bring his suit so he had to rent one for the dining room. He said he'd meet us in the lobby." Ethan couldn't take his eyes off of Samantha. She nudged him and whispered in his ear reminding him about Lauren and that she was unescorted. He offered his other arm to her. He felt like a king with what he thought were the two most beautiful women. He held his head high and gave a slight nod to the gawking men that passed them in the hall.

Lauren scanned the lobby for Caleb from the top of the stairs but didn't see him. They were about to descend when Caleb approached from behind them and wrapped Lauren's free arm in his.

"Do you think you can share one of these lovely ladies?" Caleb teased Ethan.

"I don't know, I'm really enjoying the attention," he answered laughing. "But if you insist."

Ethan gave Lauren up to his older brother's care. Caleb was dressed in a black suit and white shirt. Tiny black buttons ran from the neck to his waistline.

Lauren felt a flutter in her stomach. Her knees grew weak when she looked at his handsome face. The anger was gone and he was smiling at her.

"I'm sorry," he whispered in her ear and wrapped his hand around hers.

His surrender caught her off guard and left her confused. She didn't know why he was mad at her to begin with and now he was apologizing.

"Me too," she managed to answer.

She missed Caleb's smile and teasing. She quietly thanked the Lord for answering her prayer so quickly.

The rest of the evening they relaxed around the table and enjoyed watching the people come and go. They had a busy schedule ahead of them so when they finished eating they retired to their rooms.

Lauren fell asleep thanking the Lord for the peace he put had between Caleb and her.

Chapter Seventeen

Cynthia didn't go to church as she normally did on Sundays. She was angry with the world. She didn't want to put on a smile and pretend she was happy. She stayed home feeling sorry for herself. She was sulking in the sitting room when someone knocked on the door of the boarding house.

"Great!" she mumbled to herself. She really didn't feel like entertaining guests while Mrs. Mackey was at church. She reluctantly got up from her chair and answered the door. Two men in suits inquired about rooms.

"We have one room available right now and it does have two beds if you're interested," she told them.

The tall thin man eyed her behind his glasses making her feel uncomfortable.

"Do you mind if we have a look before we decide to board?" the older of the two asked.

"Sure." She led them to the room which was quite large and airy.

"How much?"

"Two dollars a night and that will include breakfast and supper," Cynthia told them.

"We'll take it."

The older man seemed to be the one in charge so Cynthia spoke directly to him. "I'll need you to sign the registry book, it's downstairs in the foyer." They followed her once again to the book. "Can I get you something to drink? Coffee or tea maybe?"

"Tea would be nice, thank you."

"I don't have anyone here to help with the luggage so if you don't mind, you'll have to bring them to your room," she informed them. "I'll have your tea ready shortly. It'll be in the room to the right when you're ready."

"Thank you, we'll get our bags."

The men brought their bags up then relocated to the sitting room to relax. It was very hot but the windows were open letting in the fresh air.

"Here we are." Cynthia brought in their tea and poured them a cup. She went to the foyer to look at the registry. She blinked hard to see if she was reading it correctly. *Henry Bailey* and *Alex Prather.* She returned to the sitting room.

"More tea gentlemen?" she asked sweetly.

"That would be nice." Bailey held his cup out for her.

She swayed her hips as she moved to refill his cup. "I noticed your last name is Bailey. Are you related to a Lauren Bailey by any chance?" Alex almost choked on his tea when she asked him about Lauren. "Oh my! Are you alright?" Cynthia handed Alex a napkin.

"Do you know her?" Bailey asked.

"Yes, she's been staying with the Whitworth's for the past couple of months. She's not there right now; she went to Ellington with one of the boys for a test or something. She should be back in a few days. You must be related?"

"I'm her uncle, soon to be her husband." He stood up and approached her. "But, we don't want to let her in on that little secret." He smiled at Cynthia and tapped the tip of her nose with his finger. "I want to surprise her."

"I understand." Cynthia once again felt hope for her and Caleb.

"How far is it to Ellington?" he asked her.

"I think it's about a six hour ride by stage. They left yesterday." She couldn't believe her good fortune.

"We'll only need the room for one night. Would you be so kind and show us where the livery is? I would like rent a couple of horses for tomorrow."

****

Caleb exited the bedroom dressed only in his pants. He ordered coffee the night before to be delivered to the room. He came out to get a cup and noticed Ethan was dressed in his suit ready to go out somewhere.

"Where're you headed so dressed up?" Caleb asked while he poured his coffee. "Your test isn't until tomorrow."

"The girls and I are going to church." He looked at Caleb for his reaction. "You're welcome to come with us if you'd like."

Caleb had noticed a change in Ethan over the past couple of weeks. He wondered if the bible he received for his birthday and going to church had anything to do with it. "No, that's alright. I'll pass." He tried to read the complimentary paper sent to their room. He looked at the words but didn't see them. He wanted to ask Ethan what was going on between him and Lauren. He didn't know how to bring up the subject. He decided now was a good time while they were alone. "Do you love Lauren?" he blurted clumsily.

"Yes, I do." Ethan answered without hesitation.

"Then why are you leading Samantha on like you do? You treat her like..."

"Caleb," Ethan interrupted him, "I do love Lauren. She is one of my dearest friends but I'm *in love* with Samantha. I want to marry her someday."

Caleb's stone face softened when Ethan gave him his answer. Without realizing it he let out a deep sigh.

"Do you love Lauren?" Ethan asked his older brother already knowing the answer.

Caleb didn't answer him right away, when he did it wasn't the answer Ethan was hoping for. "No, I was just concerned for Samantha. Go on now. Get to church." Caleb wanted to be alone to ponder on what he just learned. He pretended to be reading the paper.

Ethan shook his head at his brother. He wondered if Caleb would let Lauren leave because of his stubborn pride. "*You're a fool Caleb Whitworth,*" he thought to himself as he left the room.

The trio walked two blocks to the church admiring the architecture. The church was a large brick building with wide steps leading to three sets of double doors. Large pillars held up the roof engraved with angels blowing long trumpets. When they entered the building they marveled at the beautiful stained glass windows. Each one portrayed a story from the bible.

They enjoyed the service and felt welcomed by the regular attendees. They were invited to lunch by a couple families. They didn't want to go without Caleb so they kindly declined.

When they returned to the hotel Caleb was in the lobby waiting for them. "There you are! I thought I'd have to send a posse after you."

He was in a good mood and Lauren was thankful. His mood changes kept her on pins and needles.

"I have a surprise for lunch." The man working behind the lobby desk handed him a large basket full of food and drinks. "I found the nicest park and thought we could have a picnic." He smiled like a little boy trying to please his mother.

He was right; the park was well manicured with soft green grass and patches of flower gardens. Vendors had stands set up selling drinks, pastries, and an assortment of other items. The group sat under an oak and ate fried chicken, bread, cheese, and drank cool lemonade.

Caleb excused himself after they were done eating. When he returned, he had two brightly colored kites he had purchased from one of the vendors. They played in the park like children for the rest of the afternoon enjoying the time together.

Caleb knew he only had a short time to win Lauren's heart. Now that he knew how Ethan felt about her, he was going to do what he could to keep her from leaving. He thought this was a perfect place to start courting her. He just hoped she'd be receptive and would change her mind about returning to Cape Jennings.

The sun was low behind the trees when they headed back to the hotel. It had been a hot sunny day and Samantha's fair complexion burned. She didn't feel the pain until she returned to the hotel and was getting ready for dinner. She decided to stay in her room for dinner. She wanted to dab her face with a cool cloth to ease the pain.

Lauren went to Caleb's room to let Ethan know she wouldn't be joining them.

"I should stay with her," Ethan volunteered.

"I'm not sure that would be the proper thing to do. I'll stay with her and you can visit after you eat." Lauren offered. She wanted to make sure that Samantha's reputation wouldn't be jeopardized.

"You were with my brother for a week not chaperoned and I believed you when you told me he was a gentleman. Please don't think any less of me."

She knew she had hurt his feelings and looked to Caleb for help.

"They'll be alright," Caleb told her. "I'll have dinner sent up to them."

They walked Ethan him to Samantha's room.

"We'll join you as soon as we are done eating," Lauren told them.

"They'll be fine. Let's go eat," Caleb had to practically push Lauren out the door. He was thrilled to have the evening alone with Lauren. He was going to make sure he made dinner last as long as he could.

The dining room host led Caleb and Lauren to a table for two. Caleb couldn't believe how nervous he felt being alone with her; after all it wasn't the first time. He ordered for them and they sat in an uncomfortable silence until Caleb heard music in the other room.

"We probably have time for a dance if you'd like."

"That would be nice!" She was thankful for the broken silence.

She sensed a change in him from the night before and was glad it was for the better. She allowed him to lead her to the dance floor where they joined the other couples. She brought her church dresses which were her best. As she looked at the other ladies dancing she felt under dressed.

"You are the most beautiful woman in this room, do you know that?" Caleb knew what she was thinking. He looked deep into her blue eyes with the softest expression.

"You're just prejudiced." Lauren blushed and turned from his stare.

"No, I'm honest," he corrected her smiling.

When the music stopped they went back to their table. A fresh salad was waiting for them.

Lauren said a silent prayer to herself thanking God for the meal and also to lift up her friend Samantha. Ethan was as kind as his brother. She knew she was in good hands. A smile lit up her face at the thought of the young couple so in love.

Caleb saw the tender look and was about to ask her what she was thinking about when he saw an unwanted guest standing in the dining room entrance.

"This is very nice, thank ...." Lauren stopped in mid sentence when she saw the anger on Caleb's face. He was looking past her. She turned to see who had caught his attention. Bailey's dark eyes were scanning the room. His eyes locked on her as soon as she saw him.

She quickly turned to look to Caleb for help. Her eyes were wide with fear and her heart pumped so hard she could hear the blood rushing through her ears. "Caleb?" Her plea was so soft he barely heard her speak his name.

As Bailey approached their table Caleb got up and stood protectively next to Lauren. She was frozen where she sat. She couldn't look at her uncle.

"He can't hurt you anymore," he assured her. He placed a hand on her shoulder for security.

"You!" Bailey hissed when he was close enough to confront Caleb. "Why you lying son of a...."

"Mr. Bailey!" Caleb quickly stopped his verbal assault. "You will *not* make a scene." Bailey's face was red with anger as he tried to control his temper. "We'll leave here before this conversation goes any further." Caleb challenged him with his eyes. "I am in room 214. Meet me there in an hour."

"So you can run again?" Bailey accused.

"I assure you, we will be there." Caleb helped Lauren to her feet. She was so scared she was trembling. Caleb had to support her to keep her from collapsing.

Lauren couldn't look at her uncle as she tried to concentrate on walking. Caleb held her close to his side. As they were departing they met their waiter as he was delivering their dinner.

"My wife isn't feeling well," he explained. "If you don't mind, please allow the gentleman in the gray suit to enjoy the meal. If I'm not mistaken, he's not traveling alone so leave both plates."

"Yes sir," the waiter answered.

"Please put the bill on the Whitworth account."

After his final instructions for the waiter he helped Lauren to his room. By the time they arrived she could hardly breathe. She shook uncontrollably.

Caleb helped her to a chair and kneeled down in front of her. "Lauren, look at me." Caleb's voice was harsh as he tried to gain her attention. She was as white as a sheet and her breathing was short gasps. He shook her shoulders trying to get her attention. She finally looked at him trying to focus on what he was saying to her.

"Look at me." His tone had softened. "You need to settle down. He can't hurt you or take you away. We're married remember?" He was whispering to her gently and had her face cradled in his hands. He was so intent on getting her calm he didn't hear Ethan enter the room.

"Caleb? What's wrong? Is she hurt?" Ethan asked panicked.

"How long have you been there?" Caleb asked.

Ethan walked over to them and looked at Lauren. She was pale and trembling. "What's going on?" he demanded.

"It's a long story," Caleb told him.

"I suggest you start at the beginning," Ethan said staring at his older brother, "or from when you were married."

Caleb closed his eyes and silently cursed. He really didn't have time to get into all of that. "Ethan, you need to trust me. The knowledge of this marriage doesn't go any further then this room."

"So, you are married," Ethan stated.

Caleb realized it was no use to try and hide their secret. He briefly explained the situation before Bailey came to the room.

"Now, I need you to get the hotel manager. The constable wouldn't be a bad idea either. Without proof of our marriage I don't think Bailey is going to leave without a fight."

"Alright," Ethan agreed. He left quickly to find the help Caleb requested.

Caleb sat in front of Lauren. He held her hands in his. "How are you holding up?" he asked her.

"I'm scared. We don't have any proof and your family can't even vouch for us." Her eyes confirmed her fear and it broke Caleb's heart. He wanted her to know she was safe with him. "Do you think any of the married couples in this hotel have their marriage certificates with them?" he asked smiling.

"No," she whispered.

Before he could say another word Ethan entered the room with the hotel manager and a constable. Caleb quickly explained the situation and wanted to make sure his wife would be safe during their stay.

"Mr. Whitworth, you have our complete cooperation in this matter. We'll wait with you and make it clear to him he is not welcomed in this hotel," the manager assured him.

A hard knock; almost a pounding on the door made Lauren jump to her feet.

"Get the door, Ethan." Caleb stood next to his wife and put his arm around her shoulder to give her strength.

"Get out of my way!"

Lauren recognized her uncle's gruff, booming voice. She took a deep breath. *"Give me strength Lord."*

Bailey and Prather entered the room. They stopped short when they saw the constable and manager. "What's this?" he demanded. "If you think you can stop me from taking my niece, you better think twice! This man lied to me in Hadley. He knew I was looking for my niece! The whole time he was hiding her in the back of his wagon!"

"I didn't know she was there until I was well on my way home." Caleb stood at least a foot taller than Bailey, but his height didn't stop the man from advancing. "She's my wife; you have no reason for being here."

Bailey stopped in his tracks. If this was true, he could no longer claim her as his ward or her money. "I'm sure you can prove it?" Bailey spit.

"I don't need to prove anything to you Bailey but, if you want it so badly get it yourself. We were married in Jenkins and the hotel owner and his wife were our witnesses. You can head back there and ask yourself."

"You killed my parents and spent all the money they left me. If you think you'll gain anything by taking me with you; you're wrong." Lauren suddenly found her voice. She faced her uncle with courage she knew only came from God. "If you want *proof* – you can contact Mr. Hobbs. He had to sell everything to pay off your debt and that still wasn't enough. I have nothing! Nothing thanks to you!"

The news of her financial state hit him like a blow to the stomach. "You're a liar, just like him!" he shouted as he pointed at Caleb.

"Contact Hobbs," she told him again. She faced the hotel manager. "Sir, if this man secured rooms at your hotel be sure to get payment before he leaves." Lauren's comment was the snapping point. He flew at her but Ethan tackled him to the ground.

Prather froze where he stood when the constable turned his attention on him. "Stay where you are," the constable warned him.

Caleb pulled Bailey to his feet by his suit jacket and held him against the wall; his toes barely touching the floor. "You are not welcomed here. If I see or hear that you're anywhere near my wife or my family I'll not be held accountable for what'll happen to you," he told Bailey through clenched teeth. "Do we have an understanding?" His dark eyes bore holes through Bailey.

"Yes!" Bailey snapped back at him.

"Good." Caleb shoved him toward the door. "Get out."

The constable and manager escorted the two men out of the room and hotel.

The hotel manager assured Caleb that they wouldn't bother them as long as they were guests there.

Caleb eyed Ethan and knew he had a lot of explaining to do. "Check on Samantha then we'll talk," he told him. "By the way, thanks, for the help."

Ethan smiled and left them alone.

Caleb took a deep breath and ran his hand through his curly hair. Lauren was standing in the middle of the room in a daze. He stood behind her and put his arms around her kissing the top of her head. She let the tears flow from the bottled up emotions within her.

"He's gone Lauren. He won't bother you anymore." He held her tight.

"Ethan knows," she stated.

"Yes, he does but I told him not to say anything."

"Do you think he told Samantha?' she asked.

"No, she's been asleep. She doesn't need to know what happened tonight."

"Poor Ethan, he has his test tomorrow and now this!" She was concerned the evening's event would affect his concentration.

"Stop worrying, he'll be okay." Caleb turned Lauren to face him. He wanted to keep her there with him and hold her all night long but knew he had to be patient. "You need to get some rest. We have a big day with Ethan tomorrow."

He walked Lauren to her room and waited for Ethan to open the door. "Come on, they'll be okay," he told Ethan.

"You okay?" Ethan asked Lauren.

"Yes." She smiled and hugged him before slipping through the door.

The men waited to hear her lock it before they went back to their room. Caleb saw how easy it was for her to hug his brother. Jealousy swept over him. *"Time," he* thought to himself. He just wondered if he'd have enough of it.

After Ethan knew the girls were safe he returned to his room.

Caleb waited patiently for him. He went over and over in his mind what he would tell his brother. "Sit down," he told Ethan. Ethan sat across from Caleb. "We have an agreement, not a marriage. I married her to protect her from what you saw tonight," he explained.

"So you're just going to write it off?" Ethan asked sarcastically.

"I'm not sure how we'll end it, but you're not to breathe a word of this to anyone; is that clear? She won't be twenty-one until December. We'll work on the annulment then. If no one knows we're married we won't have to explain the annulment. Not only that, it's her reputation I need to protect. You know how society treats divorced women."

Ethan went to his room without another word. What could he say? It sounded like the two of them had already worked everything out.

Caleb didn't care what he thought, he was drained and wanted to get some sleep. They only had two more days in Ellington and he wanted to make them special. He was going to do his best to please Lauren. If she still wanted to leave after his attempt to win her heart, he wouldn't stop her. He wanted her to

come to him on her own accord and tell him
she loved him. Until then he'd hope for the
best.

Chapter Eighteen

Lauren and Samantha met the men in their room for a light breakfast. They prayed with Ethan and for his tests.

Caleb stood back and listened but didn't take part in the prayer.

Samantha sensed something was amiss. She noticed how tired Lauren looked and wondered if she was feeling ill.

When they were finished with breakfast, they walked Ethan to the university.

"Good luck, little brother!"

"Thanks, I'll need it," Ethan said nervously.

"You will do just fine. Remember, take your time and read the questions completely before answering. Make us proud!" Lauren hugged him.

Ethan took a deep breath then head toward the university steps.

"He is so nervous," Samantha said.

"He'll be fine. He's a Whitworth! It'll take him about four hours to take the test so why don't we look in some shops?" Caleb suggested.

"Oh! Could we?" Samantha asked with excitement.

Lauren would have rather go back to the hotel. She knew Bailey was still in Ellington and felt unprotected outside of her room.

"How about you Lauren?" Caleb sensed her uneasiness and wanted to do something to get her mind off the night before.

"Sounds like a very good idea. Where do we start?" She tried to perk up so she wouldn't dampen their spirits.

Samantha scanned the street they were on and saw a brightly painted sign. The name on the sign was *Notions* with a picture of needle and thread on it.

"Can we start there?" she asked. "I know you may not find anything in there Caleb but you can pick out the next place."

"You just never know. Shall we?" He offered his arms to both women knowing now how Ethan felt the night he escorted them through the hotel.

They entered the shop and Samantha's face lit up when she saw the assortment of fabric, lace, ribbons, and items she'd never seen before.

"My oh my! Look at all of this Lauren!" Samantha wandered up and down rows touching the soft fabric and lace.

Lauren found an aisle with ribbons of every color imaginable. She loved to use them in her hair when she pulled it back. She didn't have the money to purchase any. She was on this trip out of the Whitworth's generosity. She placed them back in the bin and moved on to the next aisle.

When the girls were done looking Samantha made a small purchase before they were ready to move on to the next place.

"It's your turn to pick out the next place, Caleb," Samantha told him.

"Okay, give me a minute. I'll meet you outside," he told them. The girls eyed him suspiciously. "Go! I'll be right there," he said as he swooshed them away.

They went outside and waited like he asked. They didn't have to wait too long before he joined them. He looked up and down the street and picked out a bookstore. "There." He pointed to it.

"A bookstore?" Samantha wrinkled her forehead.

"Yup, believe it or not, I can read," he teased. They laughed at the face he made; crossing his eyes.

When it was Lauren's turn to pick she wanted to go to the flower shop on the corner. Caleb bought each of them a rose to match their dresses.

The morning turned out pleasant. Lauren relaxed and enjoyed the time with them. They found a small café with tables outside on the sidewalk. As soon as Samantha saw it she begged Caleb to let them eat lunch there. When they finished eating they looked in more shops. Samantha ate ice cream for the first time. They laughed when she put too much in her mouth. She closed her eyes when the cold temperature caused a sharp pain in her temples. She learned quickly she couldn't eat it fast. When they were done with their ice cream, they continued their adventures in more shops.

Every now and then, Lauren lifted Ethan up in prayer hoping he was doing well with his exam.

Ethan entered the large brick university and found the registration table. There was a large crowd of young men standing in the lobby talking and waiting to sign up for the test. Ethan swallowed hard to clear the lump in his throat while he stood in line.

"Testing starts in fifteen minutes. Please report to room 180. It's down the hall, last door on the right." The announcement caused his stomach to turn.

"Name please," a young woman asked from behind the table.

"Ethan, Ethan Whitworth."

She flipped to the W's and ran her finger down the page. She flipped back and forth. "I can't seem to find your name," she told him. He started to panic. "How do you spell it?"

"W-h-i....."

"Oh, I see, I was spelling it wrong. My apologies." She looked at him from behind little round glasses. "Good luck, Mr. Whitworth."

"Thank you." He nodded to her then followed the others down the hall.

The room was big with long tables lined up in rows facing a wall with a large black board. Ethan assumed the elderly man in the front of the room was the professor. He handed a stack of paper and pencils to a couple of young men. Ethan found a seat near a window so he'd have plenty of light.

"Joe Comstock." A tall blonde held out his hand for Ethan to shake.

"Ethan Whitworth." Ethan shook his hand and was thankful for someone to talk to.

"Do you live around here?" Joe asked.

"No, I came in from Clayton's Creek. What about you?"

"I've lived here all my life. My father's a doctor and his father before him…so I guess you get the picture." He smiled. "It's my turn."

"I'm a rancher," Ethan told him.

"No kidding!" Joe said with surprise in his voice.

"No. No kidding." Ethan said sarcastically. He figured Joe thought he was a country bumpkin.

"I didn't mean it like that." Joe laughed. "Ever since I was a kid I've wanted to be a cowboy and now I have the privilege of sitting next to one. I'm sorry if I offended you."

"My turn to apologize." Ethan was embarrassed by his reaction. "I guess I'm nervous."

"You want to be a doc, huh?" Joe asked.

"A vet," Ethan clarified.

"Welcome!" Their conversation was interrupted by the professor. "My name is Doctor Brighton and I will be overseeing your testing this morning. The first part of your test is being handed out as I speak. I ask that you leave it face down until I tell you to begin. Please put your name and address on the top of the page before you start. I'd hate to discover I have geniuses in here but can't find you because you don't know your name!" He laughed at his own joke helping the students relax. "The first part you will have an hour to complete. If you finish before the hour is up I ask that you turn your paper over and sit quietly until I tell you time's up. You will then have a short break before we continue. After the second part we will go to the café for a light lunch before completing for the day." He scanned the room. "If you do not have a paper please raise your hand." He paused to make sure everyone was ready. "There will be no talking at any time during testing. You may begin." Doctor Brighton made note of the time on his pocket watch.

Ethan turned his paper over and wrote his name and address on it immediately so he wouldn't forget. He looked at the words but he couldn't comprehend what he was reading. He looked around the room and watched as the others were working on the questions.

"Come on Ethan! Relax; pretend you're by the creek with Lauren. God, please help me to focus."

He took a deep breath and started over. He read the first question and wrote down the answer then went on to the next. Before he knew it he was on the last question. When he completed the test, he glanced over a few questions he had trouble with then turned his paper over. He lifted a silent prayer to God, thanking him for getting him this far.

"Time's up! Pencils down!" Doctor Brighton announced. There was moaning from some who didn't finish. "Please pass your papers to the end of your row. When I have collected them you can have a ten minute break."

"Wow," Joe exclaimed, "that was a killer." He ran his finger around his collar trying to get some air. "How do you think you did?" He asked Ethan.

"I'll let you know when it's graded." Ethan laughed. "I was so nervous at first I couldn't read."

"You look familiar; did you go to church on Maple Sunday?" Joe asked him.

"Yeah, we did. Is that your church?" Ethan believed that was the name of the street he was talking about.

"I've been going there since I was born. You had some beauties with you. Are they family?" Joe remembered the girls well.

"One's my brother's wi... friend and the pretty red head belongs to me so don't get any ideas!" He teased him but secretly, he was very serious.

"How about the four of you come to my home for dinner tonight? We'll have a great time." Joe's family had guests regularly so he knew there'd be plenty fixed for dinner.

"I'll get with them after the test and I'll let you know. Thanks!" Ethan missed Annie's cooking and thought this would be pretty close to it.

"Break is over, please return to your seats," Dr. Brighton announced.

"Good luck," Ethan told Joe.

"And to you!" Joe said.

After more than an hour of grueling questions, they broke for lunch. Then they returned to complete the testing.

"Thank you gentlemen. Your grades will be posted in the foyer after eight tomorrow morning. You are dismissed," Dr. Brighton told them.

Ethan was glad it was over and praised God for the opportunity, no matter what happened.

****

"What time is it Caleb?" Samantha asked.

"Five minutes later from the last time you asked." He laughed.

"I'm sorry," she said blushing, "I guess I'm getting impatient."

"We can head that way if you want. Maybe they finished early." He laughed as Samantha jumped at the idea and started down the street without them.

"Hey! Don't get too far ahead of us!"

"I hope he did well," Lauren said.

"I'm sure he did. He had the best tutor in town." He offered his arm and she took it without hesitation.

"I'm the only tutor," she reminded him with a smile.

"Then that would make you the best, or the worse. However you want to look at it," he teased.

"You're impossible." Lauren slapped his arm with her free hand.

Caleb enjoyed walking and talking with her. It felt so natural to have her by his side. She relaxed as they strolled down the street. He took the time he was alone with her to give her a package that was in his pocket

"Here," he handed it to her, "I thought you could use these." He was nervous not knowing how she would react to the gift.

She took the little brown package and untied the string. There were at least two dozen of the ribbons she had admired at Notions; each one a different color. She stopped walking while she touched their softness and examined the colors.

"Caleb, these are beautiful but..." she started to hand them back to him.

He closed her hand around them. "I want you to have them." He pulled at a stray curl that escaped the loose bun she wore. "You can wear them in your hair."

Lauren wanted to hug Caleb for thinking about her until the vision of Cynthia intruded her thoughts. She felt guilty about the gift and attention he was showing her. She moved away from Caleb's touch.

"We better catch up to Samantha," she suggested as she walked faster to catch up to her, leaving Caleb confused and frustrated.

He let out a low growl. She was driving him crazy with her constant mood swings! One minute she allowed him to hold and comfort her then when he tried to take a step closer she backed away. He knew she liked his company but she constantly blocked him from getting any closer. He walked behind the girls so he could think about his situation. When they reached the university it was quiet. The testing was still under way.

Caleb watched the girls from a distance. They found a shady place under a tree to wait for Ethan. They looked at the ribbons Caleb had purchased for Lauren. He was pleased when Lauren's face lit up when she found another pretty color. He was glad she liked his gift and hoped that he'd someday understand her. But for now he'd have to take it one day at a time.

The university doors flew open as the young men poured out of the building. Their ties and suit coats were removed allowing them to breathe after being shut in for so long.

Samantha searched the faces looking for her Ethan. She was oblivious to the admiring looks she received from the other young men. Her face lit up when he emerged from the crowd. She wanted to run to him and ask how he did but waited patiently until he approached them.

Ethan gave her a wink before introducing her to Joe. "This is Samantha Colby, my brother Caleb, and a family friend, Lauren Bailey." He let out a sigh of relief. "They're my team of supporters."

"It's a pleasure to meet you." Joe shook Caleb's hand then placed a small kiss on the back of the ladies' hands. Samantha blushed from the attention causing Ethan to become territorial. He moved to her side putting himself between her and Joe.

"I've invited Ethan to my home for dinner tonight. You are all welcome to accompany him if you wish. If Ethan's going to attend school here in the fall I think it would be nice for him to have a friend when he returns."

"That's very kind of you but won't that be short notice for your family?" Lauren asked.

"My father entertains all the time so our cook is always prepared to feed a crowd," he assured her.

Lauren looked to Caleb for the answer.

"As long as you're positive we won't be imposing," Caleb said.

"I promise; it'll be fine. My mother will welcome the female company for a change." He winked at Samantha. Ethan was beginning to have second thoughts about going.

"If you're sure we won't be putting anyone out we'll be glad to come." Caleb shook Joe's hand. "We better get back to the hotel and freshen up. What time?"

"Can you be ready around seven? I'll send a driver to your hotel," Joe offered.

"We'll be ready. Thank you Mr. Comstock." Lauren answered.

"Joe, please call me Joe."

As promised an open carriage was waiting for them in front of the hotel at seven. Lauren wore a rose colored dress with one of the new ribbons woven through her hair.

Caleb was glad she felt comfortable using them after the incident on the street earlier.

She allowed Samantha to borrow one to match the pale green dress she wore. She wanted to wear her hair up like Lauren's but Lauren believed she was too young for such a style. She pulled Samantha's hair back from her face and tied the ribbon into a bow. She pulled a few curls loose to accent her oval face. Samantha was pleased with the style especially when she saw Ethan's reaction.

"You're going to make me work hard tonight aren't you?" Ethan asked her.

"What do you mean?" Samantha asked puzzled.

"Come on, you saw how Joe was flirting with you," he reminded her.

"Yes, I did but you should be proud that I'm with you," she told him.

"She's got a point." Caleb sat back with his arms crossed over his chest watching the young couple. He found them amusing and was jealous that they didn't have to work at their relationship.

"You're not helping," Ethan told him.

They all laughed when he pretended to pout.

The carriage stopped in front of a large house behind an iron fence. The style reminded Lauren of her home in Cape Jennings. The memory made her homesick as she fought back tears.

"Everything okay?" Caleb asked her.

"Yes." She smiled and let him help her out of the carriage. They were halfway up the walk when Joe met them.

"Welcome!" He shook Ethan's hand. "Come in and make yourselves comfortable."

The foyer was lit from a sparkling chandelier. A round table with a vase of flowers sat on a beautiful oriental rug. The stairs that led to the second floor had mahogany rails and white spindle pickets. The floor plan was so similar to Lauren's home she wasn't surprised when the room Joe led them to was the parlor. An elegant older woman welcomed them with a warm smile.

"Welcome to our home. I'm Rebecca Comstock." She instantly took Lauren's and Samantha's hands and led them to a sofa near an opened window. She picked up a tiny bell and rang it. A maid entered the room and curtsied before her. "Would you please bring some refreshments for our guests?" Mrs. Comstock requested.

Lauren liked that she asked her maid instead of demanding.

"Yes ma'am." The maid curtsied again before leaving the room.

"I understand Ethan is hoping to attend the university in the fall?" Rebecca asked.

"Yes. He's worked very hard studying for this test. I pray he did well," Lauren told her. "We'll know tomorrow before we leave for home." Lauren once again caught herself referring to Eden as home.

"No, do you have to leave so soon?" Rebecca asked disappointed.

"I'm afraid we do. If Ethan will be attending school we have to get him home to prepare for the first semester."

"I understand. Maybe you can come back for a visit?"

She was a warm person and Lauren liked her immediately. "I don't think that will be possible; I'll be going back to Cape Jennings shortly after we return to Clayton's Creek," Lauren explained.

Caleb over heard the conversation between the women and came to the conclusion he was fighting a loosing battle. He decided then that she could leave and he wouldn't do anything to stop her. He tried to win her heart but it was to no avail. His dream of spending the rest of his life with Lauren was no longer a reality. He knew he had to let her go and it was tearing his heart in two.

When the evening came to an end they said their good-byes.

Lauren liked Mrs. Comstock and told her she would try to visit when she was resettled in Cape Jennings.

Ethan talked most of the way back to the hotel. He was excited that the Comstock's opened their home to him if he returned. The mixed emotions of his companions went unnoticed due to his excitement. Caleb was heart broken, Lauren was home sick and Samantha realized for the first time that Ethan and Lauren would be leaving. No one wanted to spoil his moment so they kept their thoughts to themselves.

Back at the hotel, Lauren and Samantha were relaxing in their room.

Lauren was brushing Samantha's hair sensing something was bothering her. "You're very quiet tonight. Are you feeling okay?" she asked Samantha.

"You didn't tell me you were leaving Clayton's Creek."

"I'm sorry you had to find out that way. I wasn't trying to keep anything from you." Lauren was sad as well but knew she had to find her place in this world. She couldn't continue to depend on the Whitworth's charity.

"Does Sally Ann know?" Samantha asked.

"No, I'll tell her when we get back." She finished with Samantha's hair and laid the brush down. "You can come visit me since you've become the world traveler. I live near the ocean; that'll be something new for you."

She tried to cheer Samantha up but it wasn't working. A single tear slid down her cheek. "Don't do that Sammy." Lauren fought to keep her own tears from spilling.

"Caleb doesn't want you to leave," Samantha told her.

"How do you know that?" Lauren was taken back by the comment.

"I saw the look on his face tonight when you mentioned leaving. He's in love with you Lauren."

"I'm sure you're mistaken," Lauren informed her. "We've grown to be good friends; that's all. I need to leave so he can also move on with his life. I don't want him to feel burdened by me."

"Burdened by you? Move on to what?" Samantha asked.

"Since he brought me to Eden I think he feels he's responsible for me. I don't want to be in his way for his future," she tried to explain the best she could.

"How do you know *you're* not his future?" Samantha asked. Tears glistened in her eyes.

"I just know. It's getting late; we have a long day tomorrow. We need to go to bed." Lauren was done with this conversation.

They embraced each other in a sisterly hug. Samantha knew by the way Caleb watched Lauren it was more than a friendship to him. She knew he was in love with her and was probably the only one who could keep her from leaving. She prayed God would remove the scales from Caleb's eyes before it was too late.

Chapter Nineteen

"Come on you lazy bones! Get out of bed!" Ethan called as he knocked on the girl's door. He was packed and ready to head to the university for his tests results.

It was extremely early and the girls scurried all morning gathering their belongings and shoving them in their trunks.

Samantha opened the door for him. "We're hurrying," she scolded. "Give us a minute and we'll be done."

"I don't know who's more nervous; you or me!" Lauren told him laughing.

"If we don't get these to Caleb in the lobby he'll skin us alive then we won't have to worry anymore so come on! Let's go!" Ethan warned.

He sent for a bellman when the girls were satisfied that they had everything. They started out the door when Lauren decided to take one more look around the room. When content they had everything, she gave the okay to leave.

"Women," Ethan said shaking his head.

"What about them?" Samantha asked in a challenging tone.

"You gotta love 'em." Ethan gave her a kiss on the forehead.

The answer obviously satisfied her because she beamed from the small sign of affection.

They found Caleb waiting impatiently for them in the lobby. He had a carriage waiting to take their trunks to the stage platform.

"Is that all?" he grumbled.

"Yup, everything but the beds," Ethan teased.

"Feels like it," Caleb announced when he hauled them to the wagon.

He gave the driver instructions and passed him some money before he met the others.

"Let's see how you did yesterday." He headed toward the school without waiting for the others.

"He's in a bad mood this morning." Lauren observed. "Did the two of you argue?"

"He had too much to drink last night. He's not used to it and it obviously doesn't agree with him. I can't figure him out. I've only seen him drink one other time and it was when one of his good friends died. Something's bothering him but he won't talk."

Samantha glanced at Lauren. She had her suspicions as to why he was upset but Lauren just shook her head at her in a warning to stay silent.

It didn't take them long to get to the university as they tried to keep up with Caleb's pace. They arrived early so decided to wait outside with the others.

"Good morning!" Joe welcomed them in a cheerful voice. "Are you ready, Ethan?"

"As ready as I'll ever be," he confessed. "Wait here," he told Samantha. "It's probably going to be a mad house in there." He kissed her hand in the same fashion he had seen Joe do the day before. "Lauren, we're about to find out what kind of teacher you are." He smiled at her before he and Joe headed in to get their grades.

Lauren paced back and forth.

"For goodness sake Lauren, you're making me nervous. Would you please sit down?" Caleb asked as he held his head in his hands. He tried to ease the throbbing in his temples.

Lauren wasn't going to put up with his rude behavior. "I will not have you ruin this for him because of your careless drinking." She spat. "Now either you go back to the hotel and wait for us or snap out of this mood you're in." Her eyes flashed at him challenging him to argue with her.

He growled under his breath and moved to another bench away from them. He'll settle the matter of Ethan's big mouth later.

****

Ethan went to the "W"'s and Joe found the "C"s. Ethan heard Joe hoop and holler pleased at what he saw. Ethan's was still waiting near the wall where his name was posted. Joe came up to him and slapped him on the back.

"I'm in!" he announced happily.

"Congratulations!" Ethan shook his hand.

Ethan pushed his way to the sheets on the wall and looked for his name. When he found it there wasn't a grade but a note written in red ink. *Please see Dr. Brighton.* His heart sank.

"Wonder what that's all about?" Joe asked.

"Only one way to find out," Ethan answered.

"Want me to go with you?" Joe offered

220

"No, but thanks." Ethan made his way down to the room where they took their test. He found Dr. Brighton talking to another young man who seemed to be rather pleased. They shook hands before the student left.

"Can I help you?" Dr. Brighton asked him.

"I'm Ethan Whitworth. There was a note next to my name that you wanted to see me." Ethan could hardly breathe.

"Indeed I did! Please come in and wipe that terrified look off your face," he said smiling. "Where did you do your studying?"

"At home. A friend of mine helped me."

"You didn't go to school to prepare?" Dr. Brighton looked surprised.

"No, sir." Ethan swallowed hard.

"I would like to know who your tutor was. Do you realize young man; you scored the highest out of the 150 students that tested yesterday?"

Ethan wasn't sure if he was hearing correctly. "The highest?"

"Yes, and this entitles you to a full four year scholarship." Dr. Brighten smiled when he saw Ethan's face light up after he comprehended what Dr. Brighten was telling him.

"Really?" He sat down then stood up; walked in a circle then sat down again.

"Will you accept the scholarship?" Dr. Brighton asked laughing.

"Yes sir! Thank you, sir!" He shook the doctor's hand vigorously.

"Classes start September twelfth. It'll be a pleasure to be your instructor," Dr. Brighton said with a smile.

"Thank you, sir! Thank you!" he said as he vigorously shook Dr. Brighton's hand.

He had to stop himself from running from the room to share the good news.

Joe was waiting for him in the lobby but Ethan ran past him and out the door. "Ethan!" he shouted after him. "Wait up!"

Lauren spotted him first and by the smile on his face she concluded he passed the test.

"I scored the highest Lauren!" He hugged her then Samantha, twirling her in his excitement.

Joe finally caught up breathing hard. "Not bad for a rancher!" Joe said congratulating him.

"Caleb, did you hear me? I scored the highest which means I get a full scholarship!"

Ethan's excitement overrode Caleb's headache. He was so proud of his younger brother. "Good job Ethan." He gave him a big bear hug. "Pa's going to be proud of you."

"All this excitement's got me starving," Ethan announced. "Do we have time to eat before the stage leaves?"

"The sidewalk café is open, my treat. Joe, can you join us?" Caleb asked.

"I'd love to but my father's waiting for me to return with the news. Ethan, I'll see you in a couple weeks. Ladies…" he kissed their hands then he shook Caleb's. "It's been a joy meeting all of you. I hope our paths cross again."

"You're going to visit the ranch, remember?" Ethan reminded him.

"That's right, so, until we meet again." He saluted then headed home whistling; pleased with the news he had for his father.

They foursome had a quick breakfast before heading to the stage. The ride was just as bumpy on the way home as it was to Ellington.

It wasn't helping Caleb's pounding head. He leaned against the soft padding and slid his hat over his eyes. He didn't want to talk to anyone so he pretended to be asleep.

They arrived in Clayton's Creek late. Will and the rest of the family were there waiting for them. Sally Ann had supper ready for them when they arrived. They were excited when they heard about Ethan's high marks. Will almost popped the buttons off his shirt he was so proud.

Caleb hung back from the loud chattering due to his head. The pain decreased slightly but there was still a stabbing behind his eyes.

"Welcome home stranger." Cynthia was at his side. Where she came from he wasn't sure. She looked extremely beautiful in the moonlight. He smiled down at her causing her heart to flutter. "Are you going to invite me to eat with you?"

"I'm not hungry," he answered. He saw the disappointment in her eyes. She never gave up on him and now he knew how it felt to be in love with someone who didn't return the love. "I need to stretch my legs. Would you care to join me for a walk?"

She couldn't believe he was actually asking her to walk with him. She concluded Bailey found them in Ellington and claimed his fiancé. She gladly hooked her arm in his. "A Mr. Bailey was here looking for Lauren. He said he was her uncle so I told him where she was. Did he find her?"

"You told him where she was?" He still couldn't stop the urge to protect Lauren.

"Yes, he said he had a surprise for her." She looked at the concern on his face and wondered if he was angry with her. "Did I do something wrong?" She poured on the innocence. "He told me he was going to take her home."

"Yes, he found her but she didn't go home with him. She's here with us. If you ever come in contact with him again you're to let me know immediately." The anger in his tone alarmed her. Caleb confused the shocked look on her face for concern. "He's a threat to her and not welcome here." Caleb explained.

"She's back?" Cynthia stepped away from him. "He didn't marry her?" She was distraught and didn't hide it. "He was supposed to marry her and take her away!" she yelled angrily.

"Cynthia, lower your voice," Caleb warned.

"No! She wasn't supposed to come back here! She'll ruin everything I've planned for years! You have to send her away Caleb." She was desperate and clung to his arm as she looked up at him. "Please Caleb, send her away."

The hair on the back of Caleb's neck stood on end. He now realized she was obsessed with a relationship that would never be. He carefully loosened her grip from his arm and stepped away from her. "I think I'll join my family now. Good night Cynthia." He tipped his hat and walked to the café.

Cynthia stood where he had left her with anger rising beyond control. Each time he refused her; the hate grew and seeped deeper through every bone in her body. She wasn't going to let Lauren win; she just had to wait for the right opportunity to make her go away.

Caleb sat on a rocking chair outside of the café listening to the excitement inside. He heard Lauren's laughter and it tugged at his heart. He had pity for Cynthia when he saw the pain in her eyes. He felt what he saw in her eyes. He needed to get away from all of them so he could clear his head. He went to the livery to rent a horse so he could return to Eden. He left while the family was still engaged in their meal. When he arrived home he packed a few things he'd need and saddled up Trinket. He left a note for Will explaining what he could and assured him he'd back to see Ethan before he went to school. He asked Jake to return the livery horse when he went to town. Without looking back he rode hard hoping that each step Trinket took would eliminate the stabbing pain that tore at his heart.

Will was ready to go home but Caleb was nowhere to be found. They looked for an hour for him before someone told them he was seen riding out of town. Will was in a fowl mood by the time they were ready to head to the ranch. Caleb's inconsideration toward the family was getting out of hand.

By the time they arrived at the ranch the excitement had died down.

Lauren was so tired she had a hard time keeping her eyes open. She welcomed her cozy room with a sigh of relief. She decided the unpacking could wait till morning. She slipped into her night gown and relaxed by the open window before going to bed. She conversed with God and thanked him for Ethan's high scores. She was sitting in silence allowing God to speak to her when she noticed an envelope on the dresser. It was addressed to her from Mrs. Hobbs. She hesitated before she opened it.

August 23, 1884

My Dearest Lauren,

My heart breaks to hear of your ending marriage. We welcome you to our home with open arms. You will be as our very own. We wait on pins and needles for word on your arrival. I will have Mr. Hobbs personally fetch you himself. My prayers are with you my dear. Write when you are ready to leave and we will see to all the necessary arrangements.

All my love,

Katie Hobbs

Lauren knew she should be excited that the Hobbs' so readily opened their home to her but instead she had a heavy heart. She loved the Whitworth's and if it wasn't for the love she had for Caleb she'd stay. She knew she wouldn't be able to love another if she stayed in Clayton's Creek. Her heart would break every time she'd see him with Cynthia.

She folded the letter and let the tears flow. She felt defeated and drained. She prayed

God would give her the strength to walk away from the only love she had ever known.

****

Will crumpled Caleb's note after he read it then tossed it in the fire. He saw him with Cynthia before they went to Sally Ann's. He wondered if the blonde beauty had anything to do with him leaving. For years he had warned Caleb not to get involved with her. When he saw him walk away with her he believed his warning had fallen on deaf ears. He was tempted to ride back to town but it was late, it would have to wait till morning. If Caleb was in love with the woman, he'd do what he could to keep them from marrying. She was trouble and after one thing - money.

The next morning Will informed Anne he was going after Caleb. She was not to worry if he wasn't home for dinner. He left before breakfast and headed to town on an empty stomach. He was too angry to eat and his imagination was running wild only adding to his grief.

Sally Ann was sweeping the walkway when Will arrived. She could tell by the look on his face, something was wrong. She waved good morning but he wasn't paying attention as he rode up to the boarding house. She didn't know who he was looking for but she pitied the poor soul when he found him.

Will followed the voices he heard as he entered the boarding house. He walked into the dining room where the guests were served their breakfast. They looked up startled by his gruff appearance.

Cynthia entered the dining room with a platter of hot cakes. When she saw Will standing in the doorway she almost dropped the plate. "Is Caleb alright?" she asked him.

"I was hoping you could tell me where I could find him." He wasn't in the mood to play her games.

"He's not here. I saw him last night when they came home but that's it." She had a worried look that seemed to be genuine.

"Pardon me," he said to those at the breakfast table. He then walked over to Sally Ann's to see if maybe he had stopped there for breakfast.

"Good morning Mr. Whitworth," Sally Ann greeted him with her beautiful smile. "Can I get you something to eat?"

"No thanks." He took off his hat. "Did you see Caleb this morning?"

"No, is everything alright?"

"Sally Ann, do you know if Caleb and Cynthia are involved in anyway?" He hated to ask her but she lived in town and if Caleb was coming in to see Cynthia he was sure she would know.

"Mr. Whitworth, come sit with me." She led him to a table away from her customers and brought them some coffee.

"Caleb isn't involved with her and never was. He's polite to her because you brought him up to be a gentleman. He would never do anything to purposely hurt anyone. I know for a fact that he's told her that he doesn't have feelings for her but unfortunately she won't give up on him."

"He was with her last night, I saw them walking together and they looked pretty friendly," Will informed her. He took a sip of his coffee before he continued. "He left without telling us and all I got was a note saying he'd be gone until Ethan left for school. He didn't say where he was going so I just assumed he was with Cynthia." Will scratched his head trying to clear his mind. "I don't know what's gotten into him lately, he's never home. He's running from something."

"I'm pretty sure I know what his problem is. Lauren told me about her plans to return to her home. I believe Caleb is in love with her. Her leaving is causing him pain. You're son is a prideful man and he won't grovel to keep her here." She leaned back in her chair shaking her head. "I don't even think he's told her how he feels."

Thinking back on his son's behavior toward Lauren brought a new light on the subject. He saw to her every need and cared for her like he's never seen him care for anyone. A smile crossed his face. "I bet you're right and I think I know where I can find him." He went to pay for his coffee.

"No need, it's on me," she said smiling.

****

Caleb stoked the fire to remove the morning chill from the small cabin. He went there to try and sort things out without being persuaded by his family. He couldn't understand why his love for Lauren was so obvious to everyone but her. He went out of his way the past week to show his affections toward her but she was still determined to go home.

He was deep in thought watching the flames grow and didn't hear the cabin door open.

"I thought I'd find you here." Will entered tossing his hat on a small wooden table. "Do you know how worried I was when I couldn't find you last night?"

"I left you a note. I came up here to get away from everyone. I need to be alone." Caleb turned back to the fire.

"Is there anything you want to talk about?" Will offered.

"No pa, I'll be alright." He wouldn't look at him. He couldn't. He was so burdened with his feelings he was afraid his pa would see right through his lie.

"Very well then," Will retrieved his hat. "I'll leave you be, but if you need me I'm here for you." He opened the door to leave then looked back at Caleb. He was leaning on the mantle gazing into the fire. Will wished he had the words to comfort his son. "Make sure you're home in time to see Ethan before he leaves."

"I will. I promise. Thanks pa."

Will rode back to the ranch wishing his wife, Elizabeth, was still alive. She would have known how to handle this situation. She was his first and only love and there was never any question on how each other felt toward one another. This made it difficult for him to help Caleb through his time of need. Will stopped praying after his wife had died. He felt guilty asking the Lord to help his son but he didn't know what else to do.

"I know I've not talked with you and if you don't hear me, I'll understand. But, my son and Lauren need you. Please open their eyes Lord, before it's too late."

Chapter Twenty

Caleb had only been at the cabin for only a couple days when he began to get restless. He chopped wood until his shoulders and arms ached. He repaired the roof that had leaked for the past ten years. He was in the process of nailing down a loose step when he heard a rider approach.

"So much for finding solitude," he grumbled under his breath when he saw it was Cynthia. He dropped the hammer and helped her off the black and white mare she rode. She leaned dangerously close as he placed her on her feet.

"How did you know I was here?" he asked while he put a safe distance between them.

"I followed your pa the other day. I was so worried about you when he came looking for you at the boarding house." She fluttered her eyes pretending to clear the tears. "I thought you were hurt."

"Why was he looking for me at the boarding house?"

"I guess he knows how we feel about each other. He must have thought you were visiting me." She ran a gloved hand up and down his arm.

"How we feel about each other? Cynthia, I don't love…"

Before he could say another word she threw herself in his arms and started to cry. "Please, please don't say it!" she begged him hysterically.

He tried to step away from her but tripped on a root sticking out of the ground. They both tumbled back with him breaking her fall. She immediately took advantage of his confused state and kissed him long and hard on the mouth.

He resisted at first but he found it hard to ignore the aroused feelings. He held her close to him as he returned her kiss. Blue eyes and dark hair invaded his thoughts. "Lauren," he whispered. A stinging slap on his cheek brought him back to reality. He jumped up pulling Cynthia to her feet.

"Ow!" she cried, "Caleb..." she stood rubbing her arm with tears in her eyes.

"Don't say another word!" He pulled her to her horse and threw her in the saddle. Her carefully placed hair fell around her shoulders. "Get out of here!" He slapped the pony's hind quarter sending it flying. She desperately hung on for dear life. He touched the tender spot on his cheek, where she had slapped him. He felt the blood her nails drew. In fear of her return he packed his things and headed for the safety of the range. He knew she wouldn't be able to find him if he stayed on the open range. They had thousands of acres where he could disappear. He doubted, even with her determination, she'd be able to find him.

****

August 30, 1884

Dear Mrs. Hobbs,

Thank you for opening your home to me. I will always be in your debt. I'll need to stay at least through the second week of September then I'll be able to come home.

Please thank Mr. Hobbs for me. If you can send me a wire or a letter with the date he will be in Clayton's Creek I'll make sure I'll be ready when he arrives.

Once again, thank you so much for your kindness.

In Christ,

Lauren

"Are you ready, Lauren?" Annie called up the stairs.

"In a minute!" Lauren quickly shoved her letter into an envelope. She scribbled the Hobbs' address across the front. She ran down the stairs and out the door.

Annie was thanking one of the ranch hands for hitching the wagon for her. "Ah, alas. You ready then?"

"Yes! Let's go!"

After arriving in town Lauren posted her letter then met with Annie at Sally Ann's. They were enjoying their tea on the café porch when Cynthia rode in at top speed. Her hair was in knots, her blouse was torn, and her face red from crying.

A man walking down the street caught the reins and halted the horse. When he helped her down she sank to her knees.

Lauren, Sally Ann and Annie ran to her.

"What on earth!" Annie knelt down next to the hysteric woman. "Cynthia! What happened lass?"

"I was riding," she sobbed harder as the crowd around her grew, "and I was attacked!"

The gasps of horror caused her to increase her performance. She tried to stand but slumped back to the ground.

"Someone get doc, tell him we'll meet him at his office! Did you see who it was?" Tim asked.

"Yes," she started crying uncontrollably, "it was Caleb Whitworth!"

"You're lying! You know he'd nev'r do anything to hurt you!" Annie knelt down and shook her by the shoulders. "Now you tell the truth girl!" Tim pulled Annie away.

Lauren had to hold her back. "Where was he?" Lauren asked trying to hide her anger.

"The hunting cabin," Cynthia sniffed. "It was horrible. His hands were all over me and he..."

"That'll be enough Miss Redding," Tim warned. He knew all too well she was lying. He didn't want her to get the town in an uproar. "Get her to Doc's. We'll have him examine her."

"No! She screamed! I can't! I'm too... ashamed." She covered her face with her hands adding to the dramatics.

"You'll do as I say," Tim insisted. "Lauren, Annie, I'll need you to ride home and get Will, I'll have to bring Caleb in for questioning."

****

Caleb rode into camp near the chuck wagon. Kent was helping himself to a plate of pork and beans when he saw his friend.

"Welcome back!" He spotted the three red marks down the side of Caleb's cheek. "Whoa, what she-cat did that?"

Caleb gave him a dark look and left his question unanswered. He sat on a stump away from the other men after pouring himself some coffee. He motioned for Kent to join him.

"Cynthia. I was at the hunting cabin when she paid me a visit... alone." He shot Kent a troubled look. He filled Kent in on what had happened between the two of them. "She has me concerned. You should have seen the look in her eyes, she's not herself," Caleb said while staring at his coffee.

"Do you think she's dangerous to herself; or anyone else?" Kent remembered stories he had heard about Cynthia when she was in grade school. If she didn't get her way she wasn't afraid to retaliate.

The thought hadn't occurred to Caleb that she might try to hurt herself or...*Lauren!* He threw down his coffee mug and mounted Trinket.

"If pa or anyone else is looking for me tell them I had to take Lauren somewhere she'll be safe."

Before Kent could answer, Caleb was on his way to the ranch. He didn't get far when he met up with Will and Tim.

"Where're you headed in such a hurry?" Will asked.

"Where's Lauren?" Caleb asked. He only had one thing on his mind and that was to see that Lauren was safe.

"She and Annie are heading to town," Will informed him.

Caleb turned his horse toward town but Tim grabbed the bridle. "Poynter, let go!" Caleb yelled. "I need to find her! She could be in danger!"

"Not until you tell us what happened with Cynthia today. She rode into town hysterical and said you attacked her," Tim told him as he continued to hold Trinket's bridle.

"What?" Caleb shouted. He couldn't' believe what he had heard. "Cynthia's lost her mind. I didn't touch her."

"How did you come by the scratches on your face?" Tim asked.

Caleb's heart sank remembering how he fell for her passionate kiss. He knew the only thing he could do was tell the truth. "I called her Lauren while she was kissing me. She became angry and slapped me." He looked at the men studying their faces. "Pa, you've got to believe me! She followed you to the cabin the other day when you visited, that's the only way she knew I was there. *She kissed me!*" Caleb started to panic. Every minute they kept him from Lauren she drove closer to danger. "I put her on her horse and sent her back to town."

"Why do you think Lauren's in danger?" Will asked.

"Cynthia begged me to make her leave. She thinks Lauren is the reason I don't love her and its making her crazy! I'm afraid she might try to find a way to remove Lauren herself."

"Let's get to town; but I'm not finished with you. I'll need to see you and Cynthia in my office to get to the bottom of this," Tim ordered.

****

Annie made Lauren drive her back to town after Will left. She needed to get some answers herself. She knew that Caleb would never do anything to hurt Cynthia or anyone else. They waited for Will on the café porch while keeping an eye on the doctor's office. Neither woman spoke being deep in their own thoughts.

"Annie," Sally Ann's soft voice spoke to her as she knelt down next to her, "you know Caleb didn't do anything. Come in and have some tea," she softly coaxed.

"Why would she say such horrible things about him?" Annie's eyes were rimmed with tears. "He's always shown her nothing but kindness. The woman's mad, I tell ya. Her mind 'as left her."

Lauren felt responsible for Cynthia's state of mind. She knew Cynthia saw her as a threat but didn't realize it was so serious. She stood up and headed down the street.

"Where're ya go'n lass?" Annie asked her.

"I'm getting restless and need to walk for a bit. I'll be back." She waited until Sally Ann convinced Annie to go in the café. Once she was inside she changed her direction and headed toward the doctor's office. She slipped inside and waited for the doctor to exit the examining room.

"I'm sorry; I didn't know you were waiting. Can I help you?" he asked her.

"I'm here to see Cynthia. How's she doing?"

"She's pretty shook up. She's resting now. She'll be just fine. You can go in if you want."

Lauren wasn't sure what she was going to say to her but needed to see her. She quietly opened the door to the room.

Cynthia was lying on a bed with her arm over her eyes. "Who is it?" she asked. She made her voice sound frail.

"It's me, Lauren." Lauren took a deep breath and prayed that God would give her the words she needed. "I was wondering if we could talk."

Cynthia scooted to a sitting position with a skeptical look on her face. "Why, you got what you wanted so leave me alone." Cynthia gripped the bed spread in anger.

"Cynthia, there's nothing between Caleb and me." Lauren spoke up quickly before she lost nerve. She felt very uneasy being alone with Cynthia. "I don't know what happened today but I ask that you don't hurt the family that's been so kind to me; they're good people. I also wanted to let you know I'm leaving Clayton's Creek in a couple of weeks."

Before Cynthia could say anything Lauren left the room. She leaned on the door and let out a deep breath.

"Lauren? What are doing here?" Tim asked.

Lauren didn't know that Tim was there. He caught her by surprise. "I was just checking on

Cynthia." She gave him a nervous smile. "I better see to Annie." She left without another word praying that Cynthia would drop the accusation now that she knew she was leaving.

She met Annie at the café and waited for Will and Caleb. The men were exiting Tim's office when Annie saw them. She jumped to her feet knocking over her chair.

"Caleb!" She ran to him and gave him a hug. "I was so worried with the lies that woman told."

"I'm fine Annie, everything is fine." He held her close. "I don't know what came over her but she had a different story when Poynter had us together. Lauren, can I talk to you, alone?" Caleb asked. She nodded and followed him to the porch. "Tim told me you visited Cynthia. What did you say to her?"

"I went to see if she was okay." There was something in Caleb's voice that had her alarmed. "Why?"

"She is not well and I'm afraid for your safety. Promise me you will never go to her alone again," he demanded.

"I promise." She now understood that the uneasiness she felt in Cynthia's company was a warning from God.

Annie and Will joined them on the porch.

"Can we go home now?" Annie asked. "All this excitement's given me a headache."

"Yes, come on Annie." Lauren put her arm around Annie's shoulders for comfort.

They were preparing to leave when Cynthia ran toward them from the boarding house.

"Caleb, please don't go. You can stay and have dinner with me tonight." Her hair was down and wild; her eyes were still puffy from crying. She clung to his arm with all her strength. "It's ok now, she's leaving; she told me. Now we can be together." Her crazed eyes were large with hope.

"Who's leaving?" he asked her.

"Lauren, she won't try and take you from me anymore, she promised. Tell him; tell him you don't love him and that you're leaving," Cynthia commanded as she ran to Lauren's side.

"Yes, I'm leaving, Cynthia."

Caleb's warning about Cynthia was unraveling before them all.

"Tell him you don't love him!" Cynthia's eyes were getting dark with anger. "Tell him!"

"I don't love him," Lauren heard herself say.

"Tell him, not me!" Cynthia pulled a small pistol from her pocket and pointed it at Lauren.

Lauren froze where she stood. "Caleb... I don't love you!" Lauren stammered. Her eyes didn't leave Cynthia's face.

"Look at him when you say it not at me!" Cynthia pushed Lauren toward Caleb shoving the gun in her back.

"I don't love you," Lauren whispered once again as she looked at Caleb. Tears filled her eyes.

Caleb's face was white with fear. His mind raced as he tried to think of something to say or do.

"See! You don't have to leave me. She doesn't want you. Please stay here with me," Cynthia pleaded with Caleb.

"Cynthia." Tim slowly walked up behind her. He spoke softly so he wouldn't frighten her. "You need to put the pistol down before you hurt someone."

"No, no I can't. I have to make sure she won't stop Caleb from being with me tonight." An eerie smile danced across her face. "He's going to take me to Sally Ann's for dinner."

"He's going to have supper with you tonight?" Tim asked. He was trying to get her mind on Caleb and off of Lauren.

"Yes!" She smiled. "He doesn't have to pretend anymore."

"Don't you want to look your best for him? Would you want Mrs. Poynter to fix your hair for you? I'll take you home and she can pin it up real pretty like." With each word Tim took a step closer to her.

Cynthia ran her hand through her hair. She let out a giggle. "I am a mess aren't I? Will she put ribbons in it?"

"Yes, she has lots of pretty ribbons to choose from." Tim slowly placed his hand on the pistol and lowered it as he continued talking. "Then she can help you pick out a pretty dress. Would you like that?"

"It has to be blue; Caleb likes blue, don't you?" she asked him.

"Yes," Caleb managed to answer. He could barely breathe.

Tim pulled Cynthia along the street talking to her in his soothing voice. He silently motioned behind her for Will to get the doctor.

"Are you okay?" Caleb asked Lauren.

"*No!*" her mind screamed. "*I'm not ok!*" Her life just passed before her eyes when Cynthia had the gun on her. She felt she had endangered the people she loved, caused a woman to go mad, and told the man she loved that she didn't love him. She fought hard to keep the tears from spilling. She needed to be strong for Annie. She could see the event had taken its toll on her.

"I want you and Annie to get home," Will told them. "We'll be there shortly."

"Yes, sir." Lauren helped the sobbing Annie in the wagon. "I need to talk to Sally Ann. I'll be back in a minute. Will you be okay?" Lauren asked Annie.

Annie nodded as she blew her nose in her handkerchief. She waited as the two women exchanged conversation then a hug. She was glad when they were finally on their way home. All she wanted to do was hide in her room. She felt a need to thank her Lord for his divine protection over her loved ones.

Chapter Twenty-One

Doctor Harris sent Cynthia to a hospital in Ellington. She was so hysterical when she realized she wasn't meeting Caleb for dinner they had to sedate her. She was watched around the clock until arrangements were made for her transfer.

Lauren wanted to stay with Sally Ann while she waited for Mr. Hobbs to bring her back to Cape Jennings. Annie pleaded with her not to leave. The events of the past week had Annie exhausted. Lauren was concerned for her health so she agreed to stay with her at Eden.

Ethan would be leaving in a few days and Mr. Hobbs was due to arrive soon according to his letter. Will insisted he stay with them at Eden hoping to extend his visit to selfishly keep Lauren there a little longer.

Caleb and Lauren spoke to each other when they were with family, but other than that they went their separate ways.

Lauren was busy sweeping the front porch one cool morning when a rented buggy pulled up to the barn. She recognized Mr. and Mrs. Hobbs immediately. Her heart leapt with joy. She dropped the broom and ran to the buggy.

"Mr. and Mrs. Hobbs!" She greeted them with a welcoming smile.

Mrs. Hobbs wanted to hold Lauren so badly she didn't wait for her husband to help her out of the buggy. "My dear Lauren," she held Lauren tight, "at last." She held Lauren at arms length. "My goodness, dear, you look tired."

"I'm fine, even better now that you're here." Lauren hugged Mrs. Hobbs again. "I didn't know you were coming so soon!"

"Do I get a hello?" Mr. Hobbs held his arms out to her.

Lauren quickly accepted his bear hug and giggled when he growled like one.

"I'm sorry to hear about your marriage." Mrs. Hobbs commented in a soothing tone. She saw sadness and hurt in Lauren's eyes.

"The Whitworth's aren't aware of my marriage let alone the annulment," Lauren quickly told her. "Please don't say anything. When we're home I'll explain everything in full detail." Lauren saw the concern in their faces. "Please believe me when I tell you everything will be fine."

"If you insist." Mr. Hobbs gave her a fatherly kiss on the forehead. They were headed for the house as Will came out to greet them.

"Mr. and Mrs. Hobbs I take it?" He held out his hand to shake Hobbs'. "It's a real pleasure to meet you." Will's friendly smile and warm handshake made the Hobbs' feel welcome. "Come in, you must be tired from your trip."

"Thank you, Mr. Whitworth for your generous offer in allowing us lodging." Mrs. Hobbs surveyed her surroundings. "Your home is quite lovely."

"Please call me Will; we don't stand on formalities here. Annie! Our guests are here!"

Annie made her way from the kitchen to inspect the couple that would be taking *her* Lauren away. She had her mind set on not liking them. The pleasant smile that radiated from Mrs. Hobbs melted her heart immediately.

"Annie," Mrs. Hobbs hugged her, "thank you, so much for caring for Lauren. She's been on our hearts for months. We were so relieved when she wrote us about your kindness."

"Ah, she's an easy lass to love that one is," Annie told her. "She's a pure joy. I'm gonna miss her when you whisk her away from here." She tried hard to blink back her tears.

"Annie, let's get some tea. I'll help you." Lauren quickly ushered her to the kitchen detecting her near breakdown.

Jake entered the house stomping his feet and brushing the dust off his vest.

"Don't let Annie see you doing that in here; she'll have your head," Will warned. Jake laughed then noticed the new arrivals. "Jake, this is Mr. and Mrs. Hobbs, Lauren's friends from her home town," Will informed him.

Jake's heart sank as the reality that she'd be leaving them hit him. "Ma'am." He nodded his head toward Mrs. Hobbs and extended his hand to Mr. Hobbs.

"Jake's my second oldest, Caleb, Evan and Ethan should be here soon. They're branding the last of the calves before winter hits," Will explained.

"My goodness! If they're all as nice looking as this one I need to speak to Lauren about leaving!" Mrs. Hobbs teased. "She must be blind!"

"I heard that." Lauren carried the tea in from the kitchen and set the silver tray on the coffee table. "I see you still speak your mind and quite boldly at that."

They all laughed at Mrs. Hobbs' surprised look when she was caught. "It's true! To think you've been here for all these months and you didn't catch a single one of them," she continued in her teasing.

"Mrs. Hobbs," Lauren whispered under her breath. She was blushing from head to toe from the woman's daring comments. "Would you like sugar in your tea?" Lauren tried to change the subject. Thankfully, Mrs. Hobbs was sidetracked as the rest of the family entered the house.

"Hey Pa! Whose trap is that out there?" Evan asked before he entered the room. "Oh, excuse me!" He blushed realizing he had been so loud.

"This is Evan, his twin brother Ethan, and my oldest Caleb." Will pointed to each one through the introduction.

They exchanged greetings and became acquainted over tea and coffee.

Lauren busied herself in the kitchen with Annie to distance herself from Caleb. She felt his eyes on her every time she entered the room.

It didn't go unnoticed by Mrs. Hobbs. She wondered if he was the reason behind Lauren's broken marriage. Lauren's husband was another mystery. She had so many questions and no one to ask. She was a cunning woman and she'd find a way to get to the bottom of her dear friend's sadness in due time.

"Dinner won't be ready for another hour. If you'd like I can show you to your room so you can freshen up a bit," Annie offered their guests.

"That would be lovely; now that I've sat down I'm realizing how tired I am," Mrs. Hobbs said sighing.

"I'll show her Annie then I'll be back to help you," Lauren offered.

Caleb and Evan grabbed their luggage and followed the ladies to the Hobbs' room.

"I'll let you know when dinner is ready." Lauren closed the door before she could be invited in the room. She didn't want to be questioned tonight. There would be plenty of time on the way back to Cape Jennings to satisfy Mrs. Hobbs' curiosity.

After dinner they settled down in the living room for the evening. Mr. Hobbs and Will focused on a game of chess while everyone else found other ways to relax.

Caleb tried to read but Lauren's soft voice broke his concentration. He sat near the fire close to the table where Mrs. Hobbs updated Lauren on the news from Cape Jennings. In just a few short days she'd be leaving them. He closed his book and started for the door.

"Where you headed?" Will asked without looking up from the chess board.

"Just taking a walk," he answered before leaving the house.

Mrs. Hobbs couldn't stay silent it any longer. "That Caleb's a nice young man. Does he have a young lady?" she asked Annie keeping a close eye on Lauren for any reaction.

"No, no he doesn't that I know of. The only two that show any interest in anyone is Jake and Ethan." Annie got up to clear the china.

"Let me help you." Lauren got up to help but Mrs. Hobbs had another idea.

"Lauren, if Annie doesn't mind, would you sit with me outside for a bit? It's rather warm in here." She started to fan herself.

Annie noticed Lauren's hesitation and wasn't fooled by Mrs. Hobbs' real motives.

"You go right ahead Lauren, I'll get these." She shooed Lauren with her hand.

"Are you sure?" Lauren asked.

"Lass," Annie rolled her eyes, "I've had more than a few cups to deal with in the past. Now scat!"

"Alright Annie, alright."

Lauren led Mrs. Hobbs to a rocking chair on the porch. She leaned against the railing staring into the night. It was a nice night with clear skies. The stars sparkled like diamonds against the black.

"God is so beautiful," she spoke out loud forgetting for the moment she wasn't alone.

"Yes He is," Mrs. Hobbs agreed. It was quite obvious to her that Lauren enjoyed the family. She sensed she wasn't happy about going back to Cape Jennings. "Why are you really leaving Eden Lauren?" Mrs. Hobbs finally asked.

"Cape Jennings is my home." Lauren was taken back at her question.

"Is it? There's nothing there for you except us. You don't want to sit around with a couple of old folks when you have a family that loves you as one of their own right here."

Lauren couldn't look at her. She was right when it came to the Whitworth's loving her and her loving them. Leaving was tearing her heart in two but she and Caleb needed to get on with their lives. She felt leaving was the best thing to do.

"Mrs. Hobbs, there are things I can't go into here and I'll tell you when we get back to Cape Jennings. Please don't press the matter," Lauren pleaded with her.

"Press what matter?" Caleb asked as he stepped into view.

"I was just asking Lauren why she was leaving Eden," Mrs. Hobbs volunteered. "It's obvious she belongs here."

"I agree," Caleb said looking at Lauren. "But unfortunately she wants to return home. Not that we haven't tried to get her to change her mind." He smiled at Mrs. Hobbs. "She's strong willed and has a mind of her own."

Lauren snapped her head up in anger. *We tried?* Lauren couldn't recall him ever asking her to stay and he certainly hadn't given his opinion about her leaving either.

"If you'll excuse me," she said as calmly as she could. "I'm rather tired and want to go to bed. Good night Mrs. Hobbs, you're in good hands out here with Mr. Whitworth."

Before either could bid her good night she was in the house. She stormed passed the chess game, passed the card game, up the stairs and slammed her bedroom door.

"Katie's been meddling again," Hobbs commented. "Check."

"Hmmm." Will studied the board. "Giving advice?" He moved a man.

"Nope, satisfying her curiosity. Check mate." Hobbs leaned back in his chair. "Good game! I better get the misses up to bed before too much damage is done. Re-match tomorrow?"

Will laughed and straightened up the table. "Sounds good to me. It's getting late boys. You have to finish branding in the morning. Don't stay up too late."

"We won't pa," Ethan answered.

"If you don't have any pressing business in the morning, you're welcome to join us on the range," Will told Mr. Hobbs.

"That sounds very interesting. I think I'll take you up on your offer."

"Very well then," Will answered "Good night everyone!"

****

"Tell me Caleb," Mrs. Hobbs didn't want to lose the opportunity to speak to him alone, "is there any reason for Lauren to stay?"

"Why are you asking me? Lauren knows she can stay if she wants."

"I think she wants to but for some reason she feels she needs to leave." She wondered if he knew about Lauren's marriage.

"Is that what she told you?" he asked.

"No, but I have a feeling," she answered.

"Mrs. Hobbs, like I told you. She's welcomed to come or go. We've opened our home to her but she refuses to take us up on the offer.

We're not going to beg." Before she could dig for more information he tipped his hat to her. "Have a good night." As he was going in the house Mr. Hobbs was coming out to get his wife. "Good night Mr. Hobbs."

"Good night Caleb." He looked at his wife wondering what had transpired. "Katie, what are you up too?"

"Nothing dear, nothing at all." She hid a yawn behind her hand. "I believe I'll turn in for the night."

She allowed her husband to escort her to their room. Though she was tired her mind wouldn't let her rest. She observed Caleb and Lauren throughout the evening. They watched each other when the other wasn't looking, and not like the rest of the boys who hugged on her and teased her like a sister, Caleb kept his distance. There was something between the two that wasn't quite right. Was he the reason she was leaving? Where was this husband she was divorcing? Why wasn't he fighting for her? What was Lauren really running from? She tossed and turned all night trying to work out all the answers in her mind. She wasn't able to sleep until she prayed for Lauren and for the Lord to give her peace.

Chapter Twenty-Two

"Thanks, Lauren for all your help." Ethan held her close. "Please tell me we'll see each other again."

"Joe's mother invited me for a visit when we were in Ellington." She wiped a tear from her cheek. "Once I'm settled I'll see about taking her up on her offer. I'll have Sammy come too."

"I'm already looking forward to it!" He hugged her again.

"Here comes the stage." Will turned Ethan to face him. "I'm very proud of you son." He cleared his throat trying to fight back the tears. "You study hard and come home as soon as you can. Don't turn into a city boy!" he teased.

"I will pa, and you know my heart belongs to Eden." He offered his hand for Will to shake. Will grabbed it and pulled him into his arms. "I love you son," he whispered in Ethan's ear.

"I love you too pa." They held each other tight.

Will held him at arms length and smiled at him. Annie blew her nose catching Will's attention. "You better see to Annie."

"Here, Annie," Ethan offered her a fresh handkerchief, "you need this need this more than I do."

"Oh you!" She thankfully took it and started with fresh tears. "I can't believe my baby's leav'n me."

"I'm not leaving just going to school, I'll be back." He smiled at her. "I don't know if I ever thanked you for being my mamma Annie, but I want you to know I love you and I thank the Lord for you."

Annie started crying harder and held on tight to Ethan. He gave a pleading look toward Lauren for help.

She rescued him as she took Annie into her arms. "Come, Annie. He needs to go."

Annie straightened her shoulders and stood up straight. "You study hard and eat right or I'll come after you!" she scolded.

"Yes ma'am!" Ethan said laughing. He found Samantha and hugged her. "I'll write often," he promised as he brushed a curl from her eyes. "Don't let one of these other guys steal you from me."

"Here." She handed him a small photograph of herself. "So you won't forget what I look like."

"How can I forget someone as beautiful as you?" He placed a kiss on her cheek then tucked the picture in his vest pocket.

"Come here little brother!" Evan grabbed Ethan's hand. "I'm gonna visit so you start looking for a pretty young lady for me," he teased.

"He'll be too busy with his school work! He won't have time for that," Jake told him.

"Write when you can, okay?" Sally Ann said while hugging him.

"Sure will, I promise." Ethan found Caleb in the crowd. The stage was boarded with the other passengers and ready to leave. "I'm gonna miss you, Caleb. Thanks for all the support you've given me with my studying."

"I'm gonna miss you too. You'll be back for Christmas break, that's not too far away." Caleb gave him a hug.

"Let me know how it goes with Lauren, will ya?" Ethan whispered. "Is there any way that you can make it work?"

"Let it be. I've tried. She wants to go home and I'll not stop her." He turned him toward the stage. "Get going before they leave you behind!"

Ethan boarded the stage and waved to his family. Caleb was near the window where he sat. "Did ya tell her you loved her?" Ethan asked as the stage lunged forward.

Caleb locked eyes with his brother as he rode out of sight. *"No Ethan, it's too late for that."*

****

A quiet group rode back to the ranch. Sally Ann was invited for dinner so she closed the café and rode out with them. Mrs. Hobbs promised to have a feast fit for a king for all of them when they returned. Mr. Hobbs was in the yard when they rode in.

"Hope you're all hungry! Katie out did herself today! Baked ham and all the fixings to go with it." He helped the ladies out of the wagon.

The men took care of the horses before they cleaned up and joined them in the dining room.

"Smells wonderful!" Jake told Mrs. Hobbs. He gave her a kiss on the cheek.

"Why, thank you Jake!" she said laughing.

"If everyone is ready I'll bless the food, unless Will, you'd like to?" Mr. Hobbs asked.

"I would." Will bowed his head and was silent for a few seconds before he began. "Lord, I know I've not spoken to you since Elizabeth died and I ask you to forgive me." He took a deep breath before continuing. "I've let my youngest leave today and I ask that you'll keep him protected and out of harms way. Be with him while we can't. Bless this food to our bodies. In Christ's name I pray, amen."

There was an awkward silence after the prayer until Annie spoke up. "What a wonderful dinner! Let's stop the sulking and eat!" She proceeded to help herself to the potatoes.

They all laughed at her, their Annie, who always had a way of cheering them up.

Lauren thought about Will's prayer and concluded he was a believer separated by anger and grief. It warmed her heart and she told herself she'd get with him to make sure. The opportunity to speak to Will didn't arrive until the night before Lauren was to leave. She found him on the porch alone smoking his cigar.

"Mr. Whitworth?"

"Hmm?" He turned to see her beautiful eyes looking so serious. "Lauren, what's wrong?"

"I wanted to tell you thank you for being so kind to me and how much I appreciate you." She tried to hide the tears that shimmered in her eyes. "I also wanted to ask you about your relationship with the Lord; if I might be so bold?"

The concern on her face was so genuine. He couldn't help it when he pulled her close and kissed her on the top of the head.

"I accepted Christ as my savior when I was in my early twenties, after I met my wife Elizabeth." He was looking in the distance as he remembered the afternoon with his wife. "It was Elizabeth who showed me who He was. In time, with her help, I realized that it was God who gave her to me and everything you see around you." He tossed his cigar on the ground and crushed it with his boot. "Elizabeth was everything to me and then the boys came, first Caleb then Jake..."

Lauren's heart leapt at the mention of Caleb. She tried to imagine him as a child. Her thoughts were interrupted as Will continued.

"I was very thankful for the blessings. We didn't have a church in town at the time but Elizabeth made sure we set time aside every Sunday morning to teach our boys about God and Jesus. We worshiped as a family in song and bible lessons. When the weather permitted we worshipped at Lake Eden. I've always felt God's presence there. It seemed the perfect place."

Lauren smiled as she remembered the same feeling the first time she was there.

"When Elizabeth died after the twins were born I was angry with God for taking her from me and from my children. I swore I'd never speak to him again." He looked at Lauren and made sure she was listening. "Then he brought you into our lives. You were like a breath of fresh air." He made her look at him as he lifted her chin with his finger. "You reminded me how wonderful God is and the many blessings I still have. I should've been thankful for the time I had with Elizabeth and the children I was blessed with through our marriage. I know you had something to do with Ethan's accepting Christ and I appreciate it. So it's you I want to thank."

Lauren let her tears flow freely as she hugged Will.

He held her in his strong arms to comfort her. "You've become a daughter to me; I want you to know that this is your home anytime you need it to be."

Lauren couldn't speak so she simply nodded her head to let him know she understood. She stood on her toes and placed a kiss on his cheek before she went in the house.

****

It was quiet as everyone settled down after dinner. Hobbs and Will were at it again over another game of chess; Annie, Lauren, and Mrs. Hobbs were swapping recipes while Jake and Evan cleaned shot guns, preparing them for hunting. Caleb went to the barn to work with Trinket.

"I need to finish packing," Lauren told Annie then went upstairs.

Annie watched as Lauren ascended the stairs to her room probably for the last time. Annie felt her pain.

"Well, if no one else is going to do something about it I will!" All eyes followed her as Annie stormed out the front door.

Caleb was brushing Trinket when he heard someone enter the barn. He turned to see who it was and saw the determined look on Annie's face. He turned his attention back to Trinket. "Leave it be Annie," he warned.

Annie walked up to him and smacked him on the back of the head. His hat flew off and hit the ground.

"Ow! Dang Annie! What's gotten into you?" He turned to find her staring up at him with fury he'd never seen in her before.

"You're what's gotten into me!" she fumed. "You're a fool to let the lass go without a fight!"

"I told you to let it be!" he growled between clenched teeth. "She's already made up her mind."

Annie saw his hurt and softened her tone. She knew they loved each other but couldn't understand why neither could see it for themselves. "She loves you Caleb."

"If she does she's never told me." He started to brush Trinket to keep his hands busy.

"Ah! She's not Cynthia! Lauren's not going to throw herself at you like she did! She was brought up to be better than that. Can't you see that lad?"

"I tried Annie. I took her to Ellington and treated her like a queen! I've gone out of my way to be nice to her." He turned toward Annie. "Why couldn't she see that if she loves me?"

"Because she saw how you were nice to Cynthia, too." Annie stated. "When Cynthia came around you allowed her to manipulate you like a puppet and you catered to her every whimper. What was Lauren suppose to think?"

"Go!" he growled. "Leave me alone."

Annie shook her head then left without another word.

Caleb tried to concentrate on Trinket's needs but the conversation with Annie kept running through his mind. He let out a growl and threw the horse brush across the barn. Trinket pranced nervously.

"Whoa boy." He grabbed Trinket's halter to calm him. "Don't look at me like that. I have tried with her but she's so, so blind!" Caleb started to pace back and forth while talking to Trinket. "I cared for her when she was sick, I saw to her financial needs..." he tried hard to put the blame on Lauren, "I even married her to keep her safe from her uncle! What more do I have to do to show her I love her?"

"Did ya tell her you loved her?" Ethan's question rang in his ears.

****

"Would you like me to make some tea?" Katie asked Annie. Before Annie could answer, Caleb barged through the front door. He stormed up the stairs taking the steps two at a time.

"Lauren, open the door." Lauren ignored Caleb's request. "Please, Lauren, open the door!"

The sound of splintering wood and a crash had the group staring up the stairs. Katie jumped to her feet and headed for the stairs.

"Sit down Katie." Mr. Hobbs warned her.

"But! He's..."

"I said sit down." This time he took his attention from the game and looked at her over his glasses. She did as she was told.

"My turn?" Will asked with a smile.

Evan looked at Jake with a pleased expression on his face.

"Well, then!" Annie said happily, "I think I'll get that tea!" She hummed as she headed for the kitchen.

****

Lauren jumped as the door crashed against the wall. She was frozen where she stood when he entered the room.

He saw the fear in her eyes. The last thing he wanted to do was frighten her. "It would have been easier if you opened the door." She looked like a frightened deer with eyes as round as saucers. "I want you to tell me why you're leaving." He softened his tone.

"Please, Caleb," she whispered. She started to shake where she stood and thought her legs wouldn't support her.

"Tell me!" he insisted from the doorway.

She laid the garment down she held in her hands and nervously smoothed imaginary wrinkles from the front of her skirt. She took a deep breath to calm herself. "Because of me," she began, "Cynthia went crazy thinking I was coming between the two of you." Now that she began she felt she had to continue. It was going to be a relief to finally get it in the open. "If I'd known about the two of you when we were in Jenkins, I never would have agreed to marry you! I've ruined everything for you; I'm sorry!" The tears started to stream down her cheeks. "I wish I never crawled in the back of your wagon! None of that would have happened!" She started to walk back and forth wringing her hands. "I've put your family in danger, caused a woman to go crazy, and…"

"So, you did think I was in love with Cynthia." Caleb interrupted her. "Lauren, I'm not and I never was in love with her."

She stopped pacing when she heard his confession. "But, I saw you kiss her at the dance and at the picnic the two of you were, so close." She remembered like it was yesterday and how hurt she was. "When we returned from Ellington you left with her."

"She kissed me and I never went anywhere with her," Caleb assured her. "I've known her all my life. She had a rough childhood and our family's always been there for her. She misunderstood my friendship for love." He tried to grab her hands but she backed away. Now that Caleb understood the hurt and guilt she'd been keeping deep within her he wasn't going to give up on them.

"Now, you listen to me. If you never got in my wagon, Ethan wouldn't be living his dream of going to school. If you never got in my wagon, Annie wouldn't have the daughter she never had." Lauren let out a sob. "If you never got in my wagon pa would still be hurting over ma's death." She was crying hard trying to catch her breath; he took her hands in his. "If you never got in my wagon I wouldn't know what it's like to love someone so much that it hurts when I'm not with her or how I feel when she walks into a room and brightens it with her smile." She tried not to look at him. "Lauren," he held her face in his hands so he could look into her blue eyes, "I am so in love with you; I will not let you leave." He brushed the tears from her face with his thumbs. "Now please, won't you tell me why you want to leave?"

"Because, I love you," she answered him softly.

He pulled her in his arms and let her cry against his chest. Tears fill his eyes. He felt relieved now that their true feelings for each other were confessed. He felt her tremble so he tightened his hold. When she calmed he sat her down, knelt down on one knee, and then took her hand in his. "Lauren Bailey Whitworth, will you marry me?" He placed a tender kiss on the palm of her hand not lowering his eyes from hers.

She smiled down at his tear stained face. "There is nothing in this world that would make me happier."

Chapter Twenty-Three

"I now pronounce you husband and wife, you may kiss the bride!"

Caleb didn't waste anytime when he was allowed to kiss his bride. In his eyes, she was the most beautiful woman that walked on earth. Her long black curls hung down her back. Her veil was draped around her shoulders and over her hair. Samantha made it for her as her wedding gift. Lauren's dress was fitted with long sleeves and the satin fabric cascaded gracefully to the tops of her shoes. Caleb's heart skipped a beat every time she smiled at him.

"I love you Mrs. Whitworth," he whispered in her ear and kissed her again.

"Ladies and gentleman, I'm proud to be the first to introduce to you; Mr. and Mrs. Caleb Whitworth!" Preacher Dan turned them to face their loved ones.

They waited for Christmas break to renew their vows so Ethan could be home. With an unexpected snowfall, they decided to have both the wedding and the reception in the café. Sally Ann decorated it with holly and mistletoe. Katie Hobbs was determined to stay and help Annie and Lauren make her dress and prepare for this day. She said Lauren owed it to her. The scandal that ran through Mrs. Hobbs' mind when she thought Lauren was married and engaged to another man at the same time almost gave her a heart attack. It took all night to clear matters up but once the truth was out, they all laughed at how blind the two had been. Caleb kissed Annie and thanked her for the smack in the head.

The reception went all day and well into the night before guests headed home.

Lauren was starved by the time the last person left. She sat down to rest her tired feet.

Caleb brought her a plate of hot roast beef, mashed potatoes, gravy and green beans and sat it before her.

"How did you know I was starved?" she asked.

"Because I saw you dance all night and when you weren't dancing you were surrounded by chattering women." He winked at her and placed a kiss on the top of her head. "I'll be back soon."

"Where are you going?" she asked.

"You'll see." He wore the devilish smile she learned to love so much.

The women Lauren considered her family, sat with her and kept her company while she ate. They laughed until their sides hurt.

Sally Ann showed them the ring Jake had placed on her finger the night before.

"Why didn't you say anything?" Lauren asked with joy. She jumped up and hugged her future sister-in-law.

"Because this was your time and we wanted to wait."

"For land's sake!" Annie was fanning herself. "My boys are all getting hitched! Next it will be our Sammy here." She gave Samantha a loving pat on her hand and laughed as she blushed.

"Did you set a date?" Samantha asked while admiring the diamond ring.

"Summer, we're going to make sure Ethan's home." Sally Ann's smile lit up her face. "You'll come won't you Mrs. Hobbs?"

"Only if you girls start calling me Katie." She tried to be stern but cracked a smile. "I wouldn't miss it." She got up and hugged Sally Ann.

Caleb came back bundled in his coat. Lauren's coat was draped over his arm. "I hate to steal my bride away but it's time to go if you're through eating."

"Go where?" she asked while he helped her with her coat.

"You'll see." There it was again, the smile that melted her heart. The ladies were smiling as well.

"You all know where he's taking me; don't you?" She wasn't sure if she liked them being so sneaky.

One by one they hugged each other then Caleb led her outside. Trinket was hitched to a sled loaded down with heavy blankets. The horse pawed impatiently at the snowy road.

Caleb helped her in then tucked the blankets around her. Heated bricks were placed on the floor to keep their feet warm.

"Ready?" He climbed in and snuggled close to her.

"I guess!" she answered laughing. "Bye!" She waved to her family as Caleb gave Trinket the go ahead to leave.

A full moon lit the way through the forest. Lauren was so excited she could barely contain the laughter when they flew around a bend. Three riders approached them from the opposite direction alarming Lauren until she recognized her new brother-in-laws. Caleb pulled Trinket to a stop.

"It's a pretty chilly night for a ride if you ask me!" Evan shouted. "I can think of better things to do on a night like this," he teased making Lauren blush.

Jake punched him in the arm making him laugh even harder. "Everything's ready," Jake told Caleb. "Good night!"

Lauren heard Jake scold Evan calling him a buffoon. Lauren and Caleb laughed as they rode away.

It didn't take long before they were in front of a tiny cabin with smoke rising from the chimney. Warm glowing light shown through the windows making the snow on the ground sparkle.

"Where are we?" Lauren asked.

"This is our hunting cabin. The girls cleaned it for us." He smiled at her when she looked at him. "Come on." He picked her up with ease and carried her inside. The crackling fire welcomed the newlyweds with warmth and light.

Lauren squeezed Caleb's neck and kissed him. "I've never been so happy," she told him.

He placed her on her feet and returned her kiss. "Me niehter." He kissed on the tip of the nose before he left to tend to Trinket.

Lauren lay awake in her husband's arms listening to his deep, even breathing. He was sound asleep. A lonely coyote howled in the distance. She felt safe inside the little cabin snuggled against Caleb. She praised God and gave Him thanks before she fell into a deep, peaceful sleep.

The next morning she woke to the smell of coffee brewing. She watched as Caleb stoked the fire.

Caleb saw that she was awake and pulled her out of the bed bundled up in the blankets. He carried her to a small couch that was in front of the fire. He kissed the sleep away.

"I could really get used to this," she said smiling.

He laughed and kissed her again before bringing her a cup of steaming coffee. "Is there room under those blankets for me?"

She held them open so he could snuggle next to her.

"Here, this is for you." He handed her a brown package.

"Oh Caleb, I didn't get you anything," she said.

"Just open it."

She untied the string holding the wrap. A worn book with *HOLY BIBLE* in gold fell to her lap. She let her hand slide over the cover before looking up at Caleb.

"Read the inside," Caleb instructed.

She folded back the front cover and read the inscription inside.

To my beautiful Elizabeth on our wedding day. I thank our Lord daily for you.

Your husband and brother in Christ
Will

Under the *Holy Matrimony* their wedding date was recorded. She turned the pages to the record of births. Will's, Elizabeth's, Caleb's, and Jake's were the only ones recorded.

"Pa wants you to have it." He watched as she closed her eyes and held it to her heart. "Will you show me…" he paused to clear his throat, "will you show me why it gives you such peace?"

She saw the longing in his eyes. "Yes." She smiled and opened the bible. "Read these." She pointed to verses that were already underlined in Elizabeth's bible.

Caleb took the bible in his hands and read the scripture. He scratched his head while he thought on what he just read. "This doesn't sound very promising. I've just read three times that I'm a sinner." He looked at the words before him.

"We are all sinners, but, there is hope." She smiled and silently asked God for the perfect words for her to help him understand His love. "Look here."

He read where she was pointing. *"For the wages of sin is death;"* He stopped and gave her a puzzled look. She urged him to keep reading. *"but the gift of God is eternal life through Jesus Christ our Lord."* He repeated the word *"gift".*

"Yes, the *free* gift. All we have to do is believe He is the son of God and that He came here to die for our sins."

Caleb remembered his ma telling him this when he was younger but he never really understood until now. "That's all I have to do?" he asked her.

"Yes and believe in your heart that what you read in the bible is truth. It's God's book of instructions for us. You'll find all the answers you need right here." She pointed to the bible. "If you want a personal relationship with Jesus all you have to do is pray and ask him to enter your heart," she quietly told him.

"I don't know how," he whispered.

"I'll help you." Lauren took his hands in hers and helped him pray.

Caleb's eyes were rimmed with tears as he looked at the woman who he loved with all his heart. For the first time in his life he felt the peace and joy he saw in her. "You have just given me the best wedding gift I could ever imagine."

Caleb and Lauren returned to the ranch not only as husband and wife but as brother and sister in Christ. In the evenings Caleb read the bible yearning to have a closer relationship with the Creator. With every page turned and every scripture read he learned how to walk closer with God.

Winter was more severe then normal causing them isolation from town. Will led the family in worship on Sundays until the weather permitted them to attend church in town. It was only a matter of time that God's word worked in the hearts of Jake and Evan and they too accepted Christ as their savior.

Lauren praised God daily for the love she found through a trial full of grief. She thanked Him for her Christian parents and the promise that one day she would be reunited with them.
Eden became her heaven on earth and understood why Elizabeth chose the name she did. Though she never met her, Lauren felt a kindred spirit with the woman who loved her family enough to teach them about Jesus. Lauren recorded Elizabeth's date of death, the twin's birth, and her wedding date in the front of her bible. She smiled when she thought about the time she'd be able to record the births of her own children. If her calculations were correct, her first born should arrive sometime in the fall. She wanted to make sure before she said anything to Caleb. For now she took one day at a time learning her new responsibilities as a wife, daughter, and sister to the family that cared for a frightened stowaway in the back of a wagon.